Game
Night

Zane Menzy

DEDICATION

To anyone who is brave enough to explore curiosity

GAME NIGHT

THE DREAM TEAM

PROLOGUE

When Callum Bradshaw met Garrick Masters he didn't like the guy. Garrick was arrogant, chauvinistic and a fucking know it all who had to be in charge. It would be safe to say that the guy was a prick. Just another pretentious git who thought the world revolved around him.

It had been thanks to Callum's twin sister—Julie— dating Garrick that he had the dubious honour of becoming acquainted with the bossy Mr Masters. Julie was a wild child at heart who had a tendency to go for dickheads who treated her like shit, and Garrick more than fulfilled her masochistic tastes.

Julie had been working as an administrator at the Tasman Heights District Council when the cocky Garrick had started work there as an HR Manager. He was a city slicker who had scored his first managerial role in the small northland resort town and he always liked to let it be known how "quaint and boring" he found living here.

Admittedly, he probably wasn't wrong about Tasman Heights being *quaint and boring*. It was only ever busy in the summer months when hordes of tourists would flood the few veins of streets and enjoy their summer holidays, camped alongside the district's golden beaches. The rest of the year it was a quiet village with a usual population of just over 3,000 people. Far from the hustle and bustle Garrick was supposedly used to back in Auckland.

It didn't take long for the handsome Garrick to catch Julie's eye. In no time, the pair began a whirlwind office romance and within a month were practically coupled up. Julie had brought him home to meet the family for their mum's birthday. She introduced him with a beaming smile, her voice oozing with pride about the man she clung to like a joey in a mother kangaroo's pouch.

Garrick had arrogantly sat at the table with the family and barked orders at Julie like she was his servant. A dutiful Julie would bounce up off her seat and run inside to the fridge and fetch him whatever he needed—usually another beer before he was even halfway through the one gripped in his fingers.

Callum had wanted to say something and tell the asshole to be nicer to his sister, but he didn't want to be rude since Julie had given everyone specific instructions beforehand about welcoming her "future husband" warmly.

It was clear to see why she was so smitten and had prematurely attached the term *future husband* to the man. Garrick was a good-looking guy. No one could argue with that. At six-feet tall with a muscular frame it was obvious he enjoyed going to the gym and probably lived on protein shakes. His dark-brown smouldering eyes, pale skin and short dark hair came together to create a look so handsome it was almost sinful. Callum himself was used to attention from women but not on the level Garrick received.

For the next few weeks every time Julie would bring Garrick along to a family dinner, Callum would sit there biting his tongue so hard he thought he might chew it off. He would whinge to his parents that Garrick was a prick and not treating Julie with enough respect. His parents would just smile and nod, insisting it wasn't up to them to interfere and that Julie could make her own decisions.

Begrudgingly, Callum agreed. He knew his sister would do the opposite of what they told her to, so the trick was to tell her how great Garrick was and encourage the pairing. Turned out that was exactly what was needed and after three months, Julie grew tired of Garrick's aloof behaviour and reluctance to become serious, and she replaced him with a new dickhead called Dion.

Callum thought that would be the last he would ever see of Garrick Masters. He was wrong. It turned out that Julie's new boyfriend was an even bigger jerk than Garrick. Julie had not told anyone but Dion got a little fist happy after a few drinks and when she turned up to work one morning, nursing a bruised eye, Garrick demanded to know why.

Julie had tried to lie about the cause of her bruise, but Garrick had eventually gotten the truth out of her. Despite Julie's protests and begging Garrick not to do anything, he had stormed out of the office and drove straight to Dion's work at the lumber yard and bowled right on up and smacked the guy in the face, knocking him to the ground. He didn't stop there. Garrick had put the boot in and left Dion with cracked ribs and a face that took nearly a month to heal.

Callum found out about this by Julie turning up at his house in tears over the incident. She was livid with Garrick because now Dion refused to see her ever again. Callum had consoled his sister through her heartbreak while keeping to himself just how happy he was with Garrick for doing what he had done.

The next day Callum had gone to visit Garrick at his home. The dark-haired womanizer had been surprised to see Callum there, frowning with an inquisitive look on his face. Before Garrick could shove his hands into his pockets, Callum spotted how his knuckles were cut and bruised, evidence of the retribution for Julie.

"I wanted to say thank you for what you did," Callum had said.

"For what?" Garrick replied sullenly. "Did I buy you a winning lotto ticket I don't know about?"

"No. Thank you for giving yourself sore hands and beating the crap out of that piece of shit Dion."

"Oh," Garrick mumbled. "No worries."

"I know Julie is probably gonna be a bitch to you at work about it but she will eventually agree with what you did so I just wanted to say thanks."

Garrick stared at him, not saying a word.

Callum smiled, nodding his head, feeling awkward. "Anyway, that's all I wanted to say." He turned to walk away.

"Hey, Callum," Garrick had called out.

Callum turned back 'round. "Yeah?"

"Did you fancy joining me for a drink?" Garrick

pointed inside. "I have plenty in the fridge. My rotten liver always makes sure there's plenty to go around."

Callum had laughed at the self-deprecating joke. He hadn't planned to socialise with the guy, but after what Garrick had done for his sister it seemed polite to accept the offer. "Sure, man. I could do with a drink."

"Cool. Come on in."

Callum followed Garrick inside and joined him on the upstairs deck of his apartment for a beer. At first, the conversation flowed about as much as a dried-up stream, but after a second beer the pair of them found themselves talking quite naturally, swapping work stories and funny tales about Julie. He knew his sister would be livid if she knew he were there, bonding with her ex, but the longer he stayed the more Callum began to see how wrong he had been about Garrick Masters. Yes, he was a snob but he wasn't a bad guy. He was a good sort who had a natural talent for listening and making you feel important.

They ended up drinking well into the evening and not calling it a night till after 1 in the morning when Callum practically passed out on the guy's couch. When he woke the next morning, he found Garrick standing over him with a glass of orange juice, offering to fry him up some bacon and eggs for breakfast. Callum accepted the hangover cure and ended up hanging out there the whole day. It seemed that without knowing it, he had made himself a new friend.

That was two years ago. In hindsight, the start of their friendship had been perfect timing. The prior six months to that first drink with Garrick had been the worst months of Callum's life and he blamed this for not picking up on his sister's abusive relationship. He had been so caught up in his own drama and feeling sorry for himself, that he had been unable to notice anyone else's pain.

His horrendous luck had started with the unexpected decay of his social group. Being born and bred in such a small town meant Callum knew loads of locals, he had many associates... but when it came to mates, he had two main ones. Johan Niemand and Tim Chadwick. Together they had been a tight trio in their youth, but when Johan's girlfriend Stacey had a baby, Johan became less available; preferring to spend his time at home. It sucked, but Callum understood why his friend would not be keen to hang out so much, and besides he still had Tim—his best mate.

Tim and Callum had been best mates since primary school. Tim was a tall gangly lad and had been the class clown who irritated everyone around him. Except Callum. Callum found his idiot pal nothing but fun to be around. Even as an adult Tim behaved like a stupid school boy who never took anything serious.

Unfortunately, Tim moved to Christchurch, hoping to cash in with his carpentry skills as part of the earthquake rebuild. Tim moving away hit Callum hard and he missed his best mate like crazy. But the pain of missing his friend was minimal to what came just two months later—losing the love of his life.

On a rainy winter's day, Callum's fiancé Misty broke up with him unexpectedly. They had dated since they were eighteen and been a match made in heaven. Everyone said so. They had been the most popular guy and girl during high school and when they got together at their graduation party it seemed an obvious and overdue pairing.

Callum's popularity at school hadn't been based on sporting prowess like most other guys, instead, it stemmed from his boyband looks. He had a fit physique with dark blond hair, sharp icy-blue eyes and a natural year-round tan. Misty too had beauty to thank for her perch at the top of the school social ladder. Her long brown hair sat atop a slim body with curves in all the right places which made her wet dream fodder rolled into a dream come true for Callum.

It had been a busy day at the café they owned and run together when Misty said they needed to have a talk when they got home. Callum had been secretly excited, expecting Misty to deliver him news that they would soon be expecting a new addition to their family. They had been trying all year and it seemed the right time now with the business starting to really take off. But no. It wasn't baby news she shared when they got home that evening. It was heartache.

In the kitchen of the home they had just bought together earlier that year, Misty explained how they were over, how she needed more from life, a new direction and a man who wasn't afraid of taking risks. The cruelty of it all was horrifying, and as she walked away with a packed luggage bag, Callum was left devastated.

Misty never said where she was going, but when Callum ran into Misty's parents in the supermarket a month later, an awkward conversation ensued where Misty's mother informed him her daughter was now living in Wellington and had gotten a job with Internal Affairs in the passport office. It seemed criminal that she could fly away to start a whole new life without him, leaving him all alone and sagging beneath the weight of broken dreams.

But Garrick Masters helped change all of that. He helped bring the sun back into Callum's life. After that first drink together, he began inviting Callum around more and more. They soon became great mates, partying together every weekend and reserving Thursday nights for *game night*. An evening where games of all sorts were played; cards, darts, board games. It didn't matter what the game was as long as there was a winner and a loser to appease the competitive beast within Garrick.

Garrick soon taught him how to move on with life. A recipe that involved lots of booze and different women. Callum wasn't a fan of sharing himself around quite the way Garrick was, but he had to admit meaningless sex had helped fight away the crippling loneliness. He still missed Misty like crazy, but the pain of missing was at least bearable.

Fun and friendship were saviours and a good distraction to the hurt in his world. Garrick showed him that life could carry on, and even though Callum struggled to move on from his heartache, it didn't stop him for being forever grateful. So now whenever Callum Bradshaw saw Garrick Masters he no longer *didn't like* the guy, he loved him as the great mate he was.

CHAPTER ONE

Callum carried a box of beer under his arm as he pressed the doorbell to Garrick's home. Garrick lived in a two-story apartment along the waterfront—Ocean Parade— the best street in Tasman Heights. The executive pad was every bit as pretentious as its flashy owner. The white-painted complex with tinted floor-to-ceiling windows gave Garrick more than enough privacy to accompany the unrivalled views from the large deck jutting out from his upstairs lounge.

Callum got tired of waiting for Garrick so he pressed the doorbell again, adding a loud clamour of knocks to get his mate's attention. Thumping footsteps from inside hurled down the stairs and Garrick opened the door, revealing himself to be wearing nothing but a wet towel draped around his trim waist, showing off his perfect body. The only blemish on Garrick's perfection was hidden beneath his curls of dark chest hair, where light scarring from a motorcycle accident when he was eighteen could faintly be seen. If anything, the light scarring sort of added to his beauty in making him have a rough edge.

"Hey, Mr impatient," Garrick said with a beaming smile.

"Sorry, mate. I didn't realise you were in the shower."

"Yeah, I try and make myself look pretty for you every games night," Garrick joked. He ran a hand through his wet black hair before scratching the dark stubble lining his jaw.

"Aww, lucky me." Callum rolled his eyes.

"Here, what do you think of my new cologne?" Garrick asked excitedly, raising his arm up, motioning for Callum to smell his new scent.

Callum lowered his face, keeping an appropriate distance. Garrick suddenly grabbed the back of his head, pushing Callum's face into his damp armpit.

Callum reeled his head back, laughing. "Gross. I don't want your hairy pits in my face."

"Fuck, your just too easy," Garrick said, smiling. "Anyway, come in." He walked ahead, leading the way upstairs to the living room.

Callum had a pang of envy as he watched Garrick climb the stairs with a masculine confidence he made look effortless, his defined back muscles and toned legs on full display in his minimal attire of a wet towel.

Once at the top of the stairs they turned left into the open plan kitchen and dining room. Callum went and took a seat at the large oval dinner table, placing his offering of beer in the centre.

Garrick scooped the box up and went and placed it in the fridge. He returned with two already-chilled bottles of beer, handing one across. "Here's one I prepared earlier for you," he said, just as his towel came loose and fell to the floor.

"Cheers for the eyeful," Callum teased, taking the beer.

"Better that than a mouthful." Garrick winked, placing the other beer down on the table.

Garrick didn't care if anyone saw him naked—he knew he looked good with or without clothes on. He went into the adjoining lounge where a pile of clothes sat on a leather settee. He raised up a pair of briefs, sniffed to see if they were clean, then proceeded to get dressed. He knelt over, shimmying the underwear up his legs, covering up his untrimmed pubes and dangling cock.

Callum may have been the same height as his friend but the similarities pretty much ended there. The dark-haired Garrick was only a couple shades away from being considered pale, whereas Callum was blond and enjoyed the luxury of olive skin, gifting him a year-round summery tan. Every inch of Garrick was athletic and muscled. Callum's body however was slim and only slightly toned. Their difference in looks was handy when going out drinking in bars. Both were good-looking in their own right and appealed to different tastes. As Garrick would often say, they were a *dream team.*

Garrick slipped on a pair of jeans then threw on a clean collared shirt. He came back in the dining room, proceeding to rummage through a cabinet drawer and retrieve a deck of cards. "So what game is it tonight, Mr Bradshaw?" he asked in a posh voice.

"You choose," Callum answered.

"Shall we do last card for a change? I'm sick of poker." Garrick sat down across from him and began to deal out the cards.

"Sure, man. Poker's fine." Callum said, opening his beer. He gazed behind him, taking in Garrick's messy lounge. The large living area which was decked out in plush furnishings usually appeared immaculate, but tonight it looked like a student flat with dinner plates scattered everywhere and laundry draped over the couch. "No offence, mate, but why does the place look like a fucking bombsite?"

Garrick laughed and put the pack of cards in the middle of the dining table before picking up his beer. "That would be because the cleaner quit."

Callum narrowed his eyes, giving his pal a suspicious look. "Quit... or had to quit?"

"The latter." Garrick slung him a mischievous grin. "Things got a little awkward after I got her to polish more than just the stair bannister, if you know what I mean?" He lowered his hand and groped his jeans-clad crotch.

"You just can't keep it in your pants can you."

"You saw her, didn't you? She was too fucking hot to not take the chance with. Or are you too old to take chances like that now." Garrick smirked. He liked to remind Callum about their meagre two-year age gap.

"Piss off. I'm twenty-eight, not eighty."

"Yep and I'm twenty-six. Still young, dumb and full of cum."

"Dumb I'd believe. This must be like the fourth cleaner you've gone through this year." Callum laughed. "Tasman Heights isn't big enough to fuck every cleaner who comes through your doors."

"They definitely come… multiple times."

"Classy guy," Callum groaned.

"You're right though. I think I'll employ an old crusty one next time so I'm not inclined to think with the little fella."

Thinking with the *little fella* was something Garrick did all too much, Callum thought.

Garrick reached into his pocket and pulled out his phone. He scrolled through the screen, eventually flipping it 'round. "Introducing, Chantal. The latest addition to my collection."

Callum looked at the photo on the screen. A pretty young blonde girl sat in Garrick's king-sized bed with the covers pulled up over her cleavage as she shot him a sleepy morning smile.

"I can't believe you manage to get photos of all these girls," Callum said. "Do they not get suspicious when they see you holding a phone up to take their picture?"

"Nar, mate. I just tell them how beautiful they look and how desperate I am for a picture to remind me of them." Garrick coughed out a laugh into his beer bottle.

"Do they know you show everybody?"

"You're the only person I ever let see them," Garrick replied defensively. "If I can't show my best mate, who can I show?"

Callum smiled. A tinge of guilt gnawing at him. Garrick freely referred to him as his best mate, but Callum had never repaid the favour. Sure, if best mate status was based solely on who you hung out with the most then it would be Garrick by a country mile, but that didn't change the fact that the best mate honour still belonged to Tim— even if Callum rarely heard from him these days.

Although Callum didn't approve of Garrick's dirty little hobby of taking photos, secretly he was in awe of it. Every woman that Garrick had ever been with was listed in what he called *The Collection*. A folder on his computer that housed photos of each of them in different states of undress.

Most photos were similar to the one of young Chantal; sleepy morning photos of their face, clutching blankets to provide some modesty. Mind you, some photos were much more revealing; legs spread, tits out revealing.

Each girl had her own file within the filthy folder. Photos were accompanied with word documents listing the type of sex they'd had, giving them a mark out of ten. His absolute favourites were in a hall of shame-fame that gave them the dubious honour of becoming one of his laptop's screen savers.

Garrick had let Callum view the collection a few times but Callum was never that keen to scroll through the beauties for fear of stumbling upon his sister. The guy was a pig but he was good to Callum so he excused the behaviour.

"You should start your own collection, Callum. You've been single long enough. Its time you jump back on the wagon, buddy."

"True," Callum said, slumping his shoulders.

"Seriously. When did you last get your end away?"

"This morning if you must know." Callum grinned, shaking his wrist.

"Sorry, let me rephrase that. When did you last get your end away WITHOUT the help of your right hand."

"A little while ago." *A little while ago* actually meant a long while ago… ten months to be exact. When Garrick and him first became friends, Callum had let his new pal talk him into a series of flings with different women. It had been good at the time, but he soon grew tired of it. Variety wasn't his spice of life. None of them compared to Misty.

"You should let me find you someone. I know a girl at work—Lisa—who would be perfect for you."

"I can do without your sloppy seconds," Callum said.

"She may be seconds, but Lisa definitely isn't sloppy. I'd only ever pass on my best cuts to you, man."

"Said like a true man whore."

"That's me," Garrick said, patting his chest. "But for real, Callum. You gotta sort those blue balls out before you…." He puffed up his cheeks and blew a popping hot breath out like an explosion.

Callum rolled his eyes.

Yeah, it would be nice to have a fuck, but it would be way nicer to be intimate with someone he cared about. He knew twenty-eight was still young in the greater scheme of things, but he was hurtling towards thirty faster than he cared for and it felt like he was starting the soulmate search from scratch. *She'll be back though.* This was a thought Callum entertained a lot. He knew one day Misty would come home to him, realising the huge mistake she had made, and when she did, Callum would be here waiting.

"How much you betting?" Garrick asked, shattering Callum's Misty daydream.

Callum pulled out his wallet, plucked out a twenty dollar note and threw it in the centre of the table.

Garrick eyed the crisp note then dove a hand in his pocket feeling around. "I'm sure I have a note in here somewhere." He pulled a funny face, fishing around. "Aha!" His hand reappeared, displaying fifty dollars.

"I don't have fifty on me," Callum said.

"That's okay, mate. You ain't gonna beat me anyway." Garrick hitched his eyebrows.

Callum laughed. "You're a cocky shit."

"Not cocky. Just self-assured."

They played the best of five rounds, talking shit and boozing their way through the evening. Garrick lost the first two games giving Callum a sniff of hope that he would take the winnings but in true Garrick style he won the final three games and took the seventy dollars sat in the centre of the table.

"Well, that's me cleaned out," Callum said.

"Already?" Garrick asked, surprised. "How come your so povo this week?"

"It's the off season, so it's quiet at the café."

"True," Garrick said, nodding. "You should have done what I said and diversified the menu to cater for the colder months and start selling soups or something."

"I've done that already, Mr Business Advisor."

Garrick smiled. "I'm glad to see you take my advice. You should do so more often. I know what I am talking about"

"It has helped actually," Callum said. "But I had to take on a new staff member and that's taken down my profits a bit."

Garrick screwed his face up. "Why have you taken on someone new during the quieter trading time? That's just fucking mental."

"It's a favour for Julie."

"Julie's working two jobs now?" Garrick asked, frowning. "She should have said something to me if she was planning on doing that." The statement was pompous and utterly Garrick. He enjoyed reminding people of his managerial position at the Council. "We're not a fan of our full timers doing that."

Callum laughed. "No, not her. It's for Nicky… Graham's son."

Graham was Julie's current partner and so far she had defied everyone's expectations by sticking with him now for close to a year. He was completely different to every other guy she had dated. He wasn't a bad boy with model looks who treated her like shit, he was a forty-five-year-old accountant who worshiped the ground she walked on. Aside from Graham's age and his scorned ex-wife back in Auckland, he was probably the first good choice Julie had ever made when it came to dating.

Garrick's mouth curled to the side, displaying a look of confusion.

"Nicky is Graham's son from his ex-wife. He moved up from Auckland to live with them a few weeks ago. He's just seventeen and can't find a job so Julie asked if I could take him on as a kitchen hand and maybe train him up to become a Chef or something."

"Ahh, the beauty of family." Garrick smiled, taking a sip on his beer.

"Yeah. He isn't too bad. He's ten minutes early for every shift and seems genuinely interested to learn."

"Good stuff." Garrick sniggered. "I can't believe Julie is a step mummy. She kept that one quiet at work."

Callum chuckled. "You could say it's a bit of a sore spot for her. I think she's worried if she tells people she has a seventeen-year-old step son, they'll think she's old."

"Your sister could never be old. Too bloody hot for that to happen." Garrick licked his lips.

"Okay, let's not break the 'I don't talk dirty about Callum's sister rule'"

"I didn't say anything dirty. I just said that she's hot… especially when I used to make her clit as thick as a rosebud." He waggled his eyebrows.

Callum laughed, throwing the cap of his beer bottle across the table at his mate. "You're so fucking lucky you don't have a sister or I'd be getting some revenge."

"Ha. As if. Any sister of mine would be waaay out of your league."

"Any sister of yours would be so easy it probably wouldn't matter what league she was in."

"You're probably right." Garrick nodded, smiling. He started shuffling the cards again. "So another round?"

"I told you, I'm out of cash." Callum frowned. "Sorry."

"That's okay. You can try wining some of it back."

"Oh yeah… and what do you propose I put on the table to bet? An empty fucking beer bottle?"

Garrick looked around the room before slowly nodding. "How about offering your services as my cleaner. The place needs one badly."

Callum laughed. "Piss off. You have a tendency to fuck your cleaners. I think I'll pass."

Garrick leant over and patted Callum's chest. "Trust me, buddy, you'd need better tits for that wish to ever come true."

Callum faked looking offended. "The audacity to insult my cleavage, Garrick Masters."

"My apologies… A cup."

"Okay then. How much are you putting on the table?"

"Another fifty," Garrick said flatly.

Callum nibbled on his lip, thinking it over. "Okay... and do I have to wear a maid's outfit for this cleaning job if I lose?"

"Nope. My housekeepers clean in the nude." He gave Callum a salacious wink.

Callum sniggered. "You're on, moneybags. Deal them cards and prepare to weep when I kick your ass."

CHAPTER TWO

It was another stupidly quiet day at the café not helped by the dreary weather outside. The rain pelted heavy against the store's front window, beating down with the force of a marching army. It was only 1 o'clock but the sky was blocked with concrete coloured clouds giving the impression it was much later in the day.

Nursing a mild hangover, Callum was relieved to be able to coast through the day without busting his ass—even if it did mean that he wasn't making much money. He and the cash register were both running near empty. Game night had carried on 'till well after midnight and by the time Callum got home he had barely managed to catch four hours sleep.

His lack of sleep was not helped by his recurring nightmare. The hideous dream haunted him, waking him up screaming and crying every morning. Callum was adamant that if he had Misty in bed beside him he wouldn't have the dream at all. The deadly dreams only started happening after she had left, leaving him to sleep alone.

Hugging soft pillows as he fell asleep was a pathetic attempt to replicate the feel of her beside him—her gorgeous body that felt more like a home than the house he lived in. Still, the only small mercy of Misty not being there was that she didn't have to see the way he woke up from these nightmares—a yelping, snivelling mess. It wouldn't help readjust her harsh opinion of him being a "scared little boy."

Callum let his tired eyes scan the empty café. The wind howled under the gap in the door, whistling like a builder hitting on a woman passing by. It seemed pointless keeping the staff on when it was so quiet so Callum went and asked his team who would like to go home.

Jess and Tina who worked front of house and made the coffees put their hands up in a heartbeat, desperate to escape the shackles of work. Callum smiled seeing how eager they were, so he let them grab their coats and head home. This left just him and Nicky to run the store.

Nicky stood in the kitchen, wearing baggy jeans and a long-sleeved shirt. He seemed reluctant to leave.

Callum asked him again, "Are you sure you don't want to head home? It's so dead today that I think I can probably run things alone."

"No thanks, boss," Nicky said in his deceptively deep voice. "I'll go home though if you want?" It was weird to hear such a manly tone come from the young lad. Nicky scratched his upper lip which was covered with a thin strip of fluff. It looked bloody stupid, but Callum suspected the teen was too scared to shave it off in case it didn't grow back.

"If you stay that means you get to mop the chiller floors," Callum said with a cheeky smile.

"No problem, boss," Nicky replied enthusiastically.

"Okay, if you insist."

Callum watched Nicky go and fetch the mop and bucket to begin cleaning. The way the boy dragged the mop and yellow bucket to the tap looked arduous. Nicky was average height but wasn't blessed with muscle power. He had quite a skinny frame, not uncommon with boys his age who didn't seem to put meat on their bones 'till hitting their twenties.

Callum was about to go sit in the office and go over the cash books but the sound of the door opening made him whip his head around to see who his next customer was.

Garrick.

"Hey, mate," Callum said, pleased to see his friend turn up. "You've picked a good day. You get to sit wherever you want."

Garrick looked around the empty café. "Looks like it."

"What can I getcha?"

"Nothing for me, pal. I was just coming in to see if you're free tonight?"

"I think you know the answer to that." Callum's social life revolved around Garrick.

"Brilliant." Garrick's face lit up like he was pondering possibilities. "I have a date with Sherry... the Council's new management accountant."

"The redhead you were telling me about?"

"That's the one. She said that she was keen to have a drink with me after work but apparently she has a friend staying with her so she would need to bring her along too."

"Let me guess," Callum groaned. "I am needed to entertain the friend so you can work your magic?"

"Got it in one," Garrick said. He looked over Callum's shoulder through to the kitchen and in a loud voice said, "Who's this poor guy you've got working his fingers to the bone?"

Callum turned around to see Nicky standing with a vacant look on his young face. "This is my newest employee, Nicky."

"Kia ora, Nicky," Garrick said. He walked around the counter through to the kitchen to shake the boys hand. "I'm Garrick, Callum's best mate."

"Nice to meet you," Nicky said, putting his hand out.

Garrick gripped the boy's hand— giving one firm shake, up and down, like a karate chop.

"Have you moved back from Christchurch?" Nicky asked innocently, confusing Garrick with the stories he had heard about Tim—Callum's *official* best mate.

"What?" Garrick frowned, looking back at Callum. His eyes darted sideways and he nodded knowingly, like he was late at getting a joke. He laughed like it was nothing and turned back to face Nicky. "Nar, I'm his *other* best mate."

Callum cringed internally.

"I hope you hit Callum up for a wage rise since you're doing all the real work," Garrick said, pointing at the mop and bucket.

Nicky mumbled a soft laugh. "I don't mind. I enjoy it."

"That's the spirit," Garrick said loudly. "After you're

done cleaning you could give Callum some pointers. He has his own cleaning shift coming up at my place." Garrick turned around and winked at Callum.

"I was hoping you'd forget about that," Callum groaned.

"No way. The place is festering nicely, waiting for you to come give it a spring clean."

"It will have to wait if I'm coming to join you for this double date." Callum walked over to stand with Nicky and Garrick in the kitchen. "Where are we going?"

"Just come to mine around six and we can go from there," Garrick said.

"Have you got a date, boss?" Nicky asked.

"Apparently so."

"Is she hot?" Nicky's voice came out excitedly.

"Not a clue. It's a blind date to help this player out," Callum said, jabbing Garrick playfully in the side.

"Awesome," Nicky said, nodding his head. "Wish I could score a date."

Garrick patted Nicky's shoulder. "A handsome lad like you should have the birds lining up."

"Not exactly," Nicky mumbled.

"Just wait for the summer, there'll be more pretty girls here than you can shake a stick at. You'll get plenty of action then," Garrick said sleazily.

"Ya reckon?" Nicky's eyes bugged hopefully.

"Yep," Callum agreed. "Tasman Heights may seem lame now but you wait for summer and all the tourists."

"True," Nicky's voice floated almost dreamily.

"You should make Callum bring you around for a games night with him one time. Who knows, I may know a cougar or two who wants to dine on some teen meat," Garrick said.

"That'd be awesome!" Nicky answered.

The way he said it told Callum that the lad mustn't have been having the most exciting social life since arriving in town. "Yeah, maybe I can bring you along one night. Get you out of the nest for a few hours." Callum flicked a quick glare towards Garrick. "No cougars though. Graham would kill me if he found out I was setting up his baby boy with older women."

"Don't be a party pooper," Garrick said. "My first time was with an older bird. She taught me loads of tricks. It's only right we find some bored housewife to pass on carnal secrets to young Nicky here."

Nicky's face began to burn with a rosy blush, confirming Callum's suspicion that the boy was most likely a virgin.

"Sorry about him, Nicky," Callum said. "Garrick here is still going through puberty."

"Sorry, buddy but my balls dropped years ago," Garrick said. "On your sister's face."

Nicky snorted with laughter while Callum tried holding his in. "Right, nympho. Get back to work and I'll come 'round to your place tonight."

"Alright, alright. I know when I'm not wanted," Garrick joked. He reached into his pocket, retrieving his wallet. He opened it up and pulled out a twenty dollar note and handed it across to Callum.

"What's this for?" Callum asked, reluctant to take the money.

"I finish work later than you so I was wondering if you could use this to get me some rubbers for tonight," Garrick said. He saw the way Callum stared back blankly. "I'm all out."

"That's no surprise," Callum muttered, not keen to be used as a sex-shield mule.

"Please?" You don't want me going in without a raincoat." Garrick looked down at his crotch. "Can you imagine me as a father?"

"Yep. Useless." Callum grinned. "Besides, what makes you think this Sherry will even let you go anywhere near her."

"Have you seen me?" Garrick pulled a face that was half joking, half serious.

"Unfortunately I have," Callum teased.

"Be a pal." Garrick gave his most adorable look, waving the money.

"Okay. Fine," Callum sighed, taking the cash and putting it in his pocket.

"Good man." Garrick nodded. "Remember, extra-large."

Callum rolled his eyes at his mate's obvious response. "Extra-large? I didn't realise the condoms were for your ego." Garrick laughed. "Nope. Extra-large for my *cock*." He emphasised the word cock with lecherous intent. "You can measure it with your mouth if you don't believe me."

Nicky sniggered, enjoying the pair's smutty banter.

Callum grimaced. "Uh, no thanks, homo."

"Rightio," Garrick said, unfazed. "I'll see you tonight, *bestie*." He gave a sly wink and walked away.

CHAPTER THREE

Callum slipped on a suitably smart casual shirt to match his slim fitting chinos and made his way to the kitchen to make an extra strong coffee. Into a thin, apricot-coloured china cup he scooped two large dollops of coffee granules, needing himself a drink that would help bring him back to life.

He hated the dainty cups, but he held on to them like most things in this home just because they reminded him of Misty. She had been the one to choose them. Had he been the one to choose, then he would have gone for something solid and simple. He liked solid and simple things. They were reliable, dependable and tended to stick around... unlike dainty Misty.

Yet, like most things in the relationship, Callum had let Misty decide what cups, plates and cutlery lived in their kitchen and pantry. She had also been the one to choose how they renovated the old home. Instead of neutral colours throughout the house like he had assumed they would have, Misty went ahead and doused every room with a bright striking colour as if she were on a fucking mission to replicate a Rubik's Cube. The one that irritated him the most was the purple lounge. Each time he sat in there, Callum felt like he was stuck in the belly of Grimace from McDonalds.

So many times, in the past two years, he had fought with himself to paint over it, but just like the dainty apricot-coloured cups it was a reminder of happier days. Days when he had the woman of his dreams at his side. It didn't feel right to paint over such good memories. When Misty returned—which she would—Callum wanted the place to be just how she decorated it.

Misty choosing the cups and colour schemes wasn't

about her being bossy and having to have her own way—despite what Julie and his parents would argue—because for all intent and purposes, Misty wasn't bossy. She was fucking perfect. Callum just didn't like to be the one to make decisions. He just liked to go with the flow, let others be the one to call the shots.

This laidback approach to life reduced stress he thought, and had always served him well—until it didn't. Now being left alone to run the café without Misty's help he was having to make decisions and it was certainly a struggle. This lack of decisiveness was one of the reasons Misty gave for breaking up with him. A list of reasons that was as long as the invisible blade she had stabbed into his heart that day.

Callum poured the hot water into his cup and went and sat at the kitchen table, slurping back the black coffee he hoped would help keep his ass awake for the double date he was about to endure. He looked across the kitchen tiles towards the front door; the spot where Misty had stood *that day*, yelling at him about why she needed to leave. Even now it hurt like it had happened just yesterday. He sipped on the coffee, trying to fight back a stubborn tear determined to roll down his cheek as he relived the day his world ended.

∞

"You're too laid back, Callum," Misty complained. "I need a man who I can count on and knows how to take control when it matters, not some little boy too scared to make a bloody decision and try taking a risk in life."

Callum didn't bother defending her accusations, not that that stopped her from expanding on her vicious point.

"Everything is so predictable with you and me. We meet at school. We date. We get engaged. Now we're on the edge of getting married and having kids. And apparently that's it. Nothing else. Just a boring sodding life. I want more... I need more."

He tried to explain that if that was a problem then he could give her more. He would give her anything she wanted.

Instead of pacifying her it made her laugh.

"That's my whole point right there," Misty fumed. "I want you to have a thought of your own, not constantly be told by me what it is you want or think I want. Show some bloody initiative. Some sponta-fucking-neity!"

"I can be spontaneous," Callum returned.

"No, Callum. You can't. You're a lovely guy. You really are... but you're not exciting. Everything is so safe with you. Nothing changes." She raised her arms in the air, sighing. "Shit, even the way we make love never changes. Would it have killed you to ever make a move on me somewhere other than the bedroom?"

The dig at his sexual prowess burned badly. "I touch you all the time. What are you on about? I can't keep my hands off of you!"

"Yeah. You *touch* me. But when did we last have sex somewhere other than the bed? Hmm?" She tapped her foot angrily.

He sat with a rumbling rage in his belly. He stood up and marched over to her, trying to reel her in for a passionate kiss; showing some sexual spontaneity.

"No, Callum." She pushed him away. "It's too late. I can't stay here any longer. We're through. Unlike you, I intend to take a risk in life and follow a new direction."

"But... but," he sputtered.

"But nothing! I have a life to lead and a world to see. And I'm sorry, babe, it's not with you." She gave him an almost pitiful look, one he would never forget. "You're not the man for me. Whatever it was we had... it's died. We have died."

Her tone and words made everything feel so final that it felt like the whole world had ended.

"Don't go," Callum pleaded. "Please don't go."

Misty ignored his begging, she clutched the suitcase at her feet and walked out the door, shattering everything he had ever believed in. All he could do was cry. Cry and cry. Just like the *little boy* she said he was.

∞

The only supermarket in town was busy as it always was this late in the afternoon. Families making mad dashes through the aisles looking for a last-minute solution for dinner. Callum wandered through the store, looking for the aisle where the condoms lived. He may have been a grown man but that didn't stop him feeling embarrassed about what he was purchasing.

Bloody Garrick!

He wished he had a packet of his own he could have just donated, but he didn't. The last rubbers he owned he had given away to Julie who turned up one day for a visit and got onto sharing just how she couldn't keep her hands off of Graham and how fast they were going through condoms.

"Seriously, it's such a pain," she whined. "I told Graham I'm on the pill but he just wants us to be extra careful. We wouldn't mind starting a family together but it just feels too soon, you know?"

Callum had nodded along, his eyes glazed over.

"Sure, we have money but I'd rather not spend a small fortune on throwaway rubbers if I can help it. I suppose the alternative is sticking to blow jobs which is fine for him but it ain't exactly fun for me getting pubes stuck in my teeth... and you've seen how hairy that man is."

Callum's gut had turned. To try and shut her up so he didn't have to hear any more, Callum had gone to his bedroom and came back and thrown the near-full box at her. "You can have these on the condition I don't have to hear another word about what it is you get up to with Hairy Maclary."

Julie had laughed and put the box in her handbag. "Thanks."

Whilst Callum wasn't at all open about his sexual exploits—or lack of them—his sister had no shame when sharing such details. In many ways, she was Garrick with tits. A free spirit who didn't believe in sexual shame, whereas Callum tended to err on the side of prudish embarrassment when it came to such matters.

Callum darted up and down the aisles, trying to find the requested rubbers. It was proving a losing battle. The store had recently undergone a huge makeover, doubling in size and adopting a completely new layout. Being the only supermarket in town meant that the shop had always been a goldmine and the family who owned it—the Williams—had become very wealthy indeed through the years.

Finally, halfway down the health and beauty aisle, Callum spotted shiny bottles of lubricant. On the shelves above he saw rows of condom boxes, lined up in their varying designs and sizes. He drifted his eyes across, trying to find the requested extra-large size. Callum spotted the packet he needed and quickly plucked it from the shelf, hoping to be done with this mini mission.

"Good choice, Callum" said a voice from behind.

Callum whirled around, startled. Standing behind him was a face Callum hadn't seen for ten years. A face he didn't think he would ever see again. *David Williams.* The store owners' eldest son and one of Callum's former school friends.

"Wow, David," Callum said, looking his old friend up and down. David looked just the same as he had a decade ago… lean, slight, almost on the pretty side with his black hair and friendly green eyes framed with inky lashes. "What… what are you doing here?"

"I moved back nearly a month ago and am helping Mum and Dad out with the store."

"Oh." Callum nodded. "A month ago? Gosh, and I haven't seen you in here 'till now."

"I'm guessing that means you do your weekly shop on either a Sunday or Monday?" David smiled. "My days off."

"Yep. Shopping day for me is a Monday." Callum suddenly felt nervous, unsure what to talk about to this person who had left town in a cloud of mystery a decade ago. When they had last seen each other, it had not been the most pleasant of experiences. Their friendship had ended in dramatic fashion. In fact, David's friendships with everybody ended badly that summer after he began to act fucking weird and do stupid shit.

"Mum tells me that you run your own café now and she says the food's amazing," David said. "You always were good at cooking. I remember you used to make all the guys awesome feeds when we stayed at your place."

"Thanks." Callum nodded politely. "I figured I may as well try and make money out of the one thing I'm good at."

"I see you're still too modest." David chuckled. "You were always good at loads of stuff."

"Stop it. You'll make me blush," Callum joked.

"We can't have that now."

Callum scratched his head, smiling nervously. "So... umm..."

David appeared entertained by Callum's awkwardness. "Where have I been the past ten years? Is that what you want to ask?"

"Ha. Yeah. That."

"Here, there and everywhere really. Just sort of stumbling through life as you do."

"Stumbling through life?"

David nodded, reluctant to go into detail.

"What does that mean?" Callum asked. "Did you become a street mime? Join a hippy commune?"

"No. Nothing quite as cool as that I'm afraid," David said with a hesitant glance. "I studied management at university then ended up going off and exploring the world a bit."

Exploring the world. Just what Misty wished we had done.

"True. And are you back here for good?" Callum asked.

"I'm not sure. I'm just seeing how things work out at the moment. Taking one day at a time."

Callum couldn't work out if the sentence was laced with wonder or sadness. He felt his gut begin to churn with guilt as he remembered the last time he saw David. Callum hadn't been as kind as he could have been. It wasn't David's fault that he was gay or whatever the fuck he was... but finding out the way he had hadn't helped Callum take it well. He opened his mouth, ready to offer a long overdue apology, "David, I'm—"

"*David to the stockroom please. David to the stock room,*" A woman's voice blared through the store's speaker system.

"It sounds like I'm needed," David said. He smiled, shaking his head. "It was nice bumping into you, Callum. You're looking really good."

"Thanks, David. You too. Have a good night."

"I'll try, but I'm guessing it won't be half as good as yours." David grinned, flicking his eyes towards the condoms. "Catch ya 'round… *big guy.*"

Callum offered a crooked smile, shame seeping into his cheeks as he watched David turn and walk away without getting the chance to receive a much overdue apology.

CHAPTER FOUR

The bar was busy with Friday night work drinks. Ass's and elbows crammed the joint, constant nattering and happy music mingled to create a warm cauldron of sociability. Tucked away in a corner, Callum sat in a cosy booth with Garrick and their respective dates.

Sherry was every bit as hot as Garrick had said. A tall leggy redhead who had all men's eyes on her the moment she had walked in. Her friend Dawn was pretty but nothing compared to Sherry. She had soft brown eyes which matched her mousy-brown hair framing her pleasant face.

The two girls sat together on one side of the booth, leaving Garrick and Callum to sit side by side across from them. So far the conversation had been hogged by Sherry and Dawn, prattling on about their friends back in Auckland. It turned out that Sherry, like Garrick, was a city dweller who had decided to move north after landing a more senior role at Tasman Heights Council. A senior role she said she would struggle to have scored back in the competitive city market.

Dawn apparently was keen on moving north too, falling in love with the small village since arriving. "It's just so amazing up here," she said. "I can't imagine how wonderful it must be waking up every day and having so much beauty around you."

"You must have that wherever you wake up, Sherry," Garrick said, reaching out to stroke her hand.

Callum fought the urge to roll his eyes.

Sherry playfully swatted his hand away, giggling. "Easy, tiger."

"I can be easy if you want me to be," Garrick said in a silky voice.

Callum wasn't surprised by Garrick's obvious flirts.

They had been here for just over two hours and so far Sherry hadn't given him the slightest hint that she was interested. As a result, Garrick's usually cool calm attitude had begun to give way to more blatant manoeuvres. Secretly, Callum was enjoying seeing his mate sweat under the collar a bit. It wasn't often that Garrick Masters lucked out.

"You're priceless," Sherry said, trying not to laugh.

"That's me," Garrick answered, grinning.

Sherry shifted her attention back to dawn, nudging her elbow. "Dawny, what do you think of Callum?"

The bold conversation change caught Callum off guard. He looked back at the girls with bewildered eyes.

Dawn smiled, her lips slightly droopy from her fourth cocktail. "Callum's a doll. So good-looking too."

"Thanks." Callum smiled back. *Maybe I should have bought a box of rubbers for myself.* He let his eyes drop to Dawn's breasts on show in her lowcut top. His cock twitched, stirring to life. Maybe she would be worth ending his self-imposed celibacy. With the alcohol flowing through him, he definitely began to feel weak for something physical.

"He is, isn't he," Sherry added. "Very good-looking."

Both women began eyeing him like a piece of meat.

"And what about me?" Garrick huffed indignantly.

Sherry pursed her lips, considering the question. "You're pretty too, Garrick, don't worry."

"Good," he replied.

"But not as much as Callum," Dawn giggled.

What? Callum couldn't believe what he had just heard. The night had gone from dull generic conversating to blatant sizing up.

"Each to their own," Garrick grumbled, swigging back on his drink.

"I can't believe you're single," Dawn said. "Guys like you always have girlfriends back in Auckland."

"I think you mean they have boyfriends," Garrick said, an attempt at humour that fizzled under the weight of his pettiness.

"Is somebody a little bit jealous," Sherry purred.

"Nope." Garrick shook his head firmly. "Unless he's your favourite too?"

Oh god. Callum could feel the fury attached to the question. This was the first time they had ever been in a situation where a girl was so blatantly choosing Callum over Garrick. A part of Callum was fucking loving it, the other part was curling up from how awkward it was becoming.

Sherry smiled. Toying with the question. She took a breath and delivered a hefty cryptic blow to Garrick's ego. "No comment." Her flirty eyes landed on Callum's chest, perving in similar fashion the way he had at Dawn's tits.

Garrick sniggered, failing to hide his annoyance at being second best.

"Do you work out?" Dawn asked.

"Not really. I sometimes go for a run but Garrick's the gym junkie. Not me." Callum patted his mate's bicep.

"Really?" Dawn said, surprised. "I guess I'd have to see you with your shirts off to compare."

"That can be arranged," Garrick said. "If we can see you girls take your tops off too. You know... so we can compare." He narrowed his eyes. "Could be quite a fun game all four of us."

Shoot me now. Callum wanted to crawl under the table and hide. He waited for Dawn and Sherry to lose their shit but to his surprise they both just laughed.

"Filthy boy," Sherry said humorously.

"Nothing wrong with a bit of a filthy foursome." He looked around the table. "We'd make a good team." He patted Callum on the shoulder. "Wouldn't we, buddy?"

It seemed like Garrick was on a mission to be as crass as possible, a not-so-subtle way of getting back at the girls for not bowing down to his beauty.

Sherry rolled her eyes. "Maybe you two boys could start the show and we could just watch."

"That ain't happening," Callum said bluntly.

Garrick stared across at Sherry, unperturbed. "I guess if having access to you meant sitting on Callum's face first, then so be it."

"Fuck off," Callum blurted, laughing. "Your hairy ass ain't going anywhere near my face."

"What a boring sod," Garrick teased.

Boring. Callum ignored the jab. He knew Garrick didn't mean it but it still hurt.

Dawn whispered in Sherry's ear, giggling.

"Just ask him," Sherry replied to her drunk friend.

"Ask me what?" Garrick frowned.

"Not you," Dawn snapped. "Callum."

"Me?" Callum pointed at himself.

Dawn nodded sheepishly.

Sherry sighed. "Dawn wants to see you lift your shirt up so she can see if you have abs or not."

"I don't really have abs," Callum answered honestly. "Maybe just a faint outline." He felt nerves getting the better of him. Dawn seemed like a sure deal, but he was starting to panic.

"Don't be shy," Sherry said, urging him to lift his shirt. "Give us a wee strip tease."

Callum looked at both women who sat with greedy smiles. "Okay then." He dropped his hands and slowly lifted the hem of his shirt with fumbling fingers, stopping just below his nipples.

"You have such gorgeous skin," Dawn cooed, eyeing his stomach. "I wish I could tan like that."

"Me too," Sherry agreed.

Callum felt like an idiot with his tummy exposed. Next to him, Garrick slumped back in the seat, radiating a hostile energy.

"Mmm. You have a treasure trail," Dawn said. She suddenly stood up, leaning across the table to touch it. She pressed her fingers to his bellybutton, drifting her fingers down across the whispery blond hairs 'till she reached the waistband of his chinos. "Yum." She gave him a saucy look, nibbling her lip.

Callum felt his loins flame with desire. *Looks like I'm the one getting laid tonight.* Just as his cock pulsed with a burning heat it was cooled off in wet fashion. Dawn's elbow knocked his tall glass of beer over, spilling it all down his crotch and soaking his pants.

"Oh my god. I am so sorry, Callum" She squealed, sitting back down. "I really didn't mean to do that."

He stood up, trying to brush cold dribbles of beer off him. It looked like he had pissed himself badly. *Fucking great.*

"I think maybe we should call it a night," Garrick hissed. He stood up, stepping out of the booth.

"That's probably a good idea," Sherry agreed, looking at Dawn.

"Oh, I feel so bad," Dawn rambled. "Let me find you a napkin or something."

"No. It's fine." Callum smiled at her. "It can dry on its own."

"Did you ladies need a lift home?" Garrick jangled his keys.

"No. It's fine. I only live down the road." Sherry grabbed Dawn's hand, leading her out of the booth. "The fresh air will do Dawn some good."

"What… you're going home?" Callum asked, his voice sounding meek.

"I think it's best," Sherry replied, putting an arm around her friend.

Callum's horniness made him grasp at straws and he blurted, "Did you want to come back to my place for a drink, Dawn?"

Garrick sniggered, hearing the desperation in his voice.

"Not tonight, handsome." Dawn smiled. "Another time maybe?"

Callum stood beside Garrick as they watched the girls walk away. Once they were outside, Garrick said, "Fucking teases."

Callum nodded.

Garrick looked down at Callum's drink-stained crotch. "At least one of us got our dick wet tonight." He burst out laughing at his own joke.

"Funny guy," Callum groaned.

"Come on, buddy." Garrick put his arm around Callum's shoulders. "Let's head back to mine and get you cleaned up."

CHAPTER FIVE

When they got back to Garrick's, Callum couldn't wait to use the bathroom and get clean. The spilt beer had dried on his stomach, becoming sticky and gross. The unpleasant feeling hadn't been helped by the chilly night air that had licked at his damp crotch on the short walk to the car, numbing his nuts.

"You can be the first person other than myself to try out the new kickass shower," Garrick said, reaching into the hot airing cupboard to fetch a clean towel.

"True. Is it good?"

"Fuck yeah," Garrick said, handing over the towel. "The water pressure is like a bloody bazooka."

Callum laughed. "I hope I don't lose a limb turning it on then."

"You'll be right." Garrick looked around, frowning slightly. "Right, I'm gonna go pour myself a drink. Fancy one?"

"I spose I've got time for one before I head home."

"Sweet. Rum and coke all good?"

Callum nodded. "All good by me."

"Drop ya clothes in the hallway here and I can chuck them in the dryer for you quickly."

"That'd be great," Callum said. "Thanks."

Garrick walked back towards the kitchen, leaving Callum to go have a shower. He opened the bathroom door and immediately noticed the new shower unit Garrick was talking about. It wasn't just a new unit. It was a whole renovation. He had replaced the tiles throughout, and in the corner of the room was a large see-through glass box surrounding a section of the tiles with a drain in the middle.

41

The shower had a more traditional nozzle jutting out the wall, while hanging from the ceiling was a metal disk that Callum assumed would pour down like rain.

Fancy fucker.

It was no surprise to see Garrick go for the most expensive unit he could find. He was on good money at the Council and only had himself to worry about. Why wouldn't you splash out and treat yourself to the finer things in life. Callum wished he could afford such nice things. The café had failed to live up to its potential, probably not helped by him running it alone. Misty had been the business-minded one. Not him.

If he had the balls then he would probably quite happily part with the bloody thing. Running a business alone didn't feel worth the stress, but like every other thing in his life, he held onto it just on the chance Misty might come back to him.

Not might. She will.

Others would say it was wishful thinking but Callum could feel it in his bones. Misty would come back. One day. Aside from the fact she would come to her senses and remember the love she actually had for Callum, Misty was a true born n' bred local. Tasman Height's folk may leave for a while, but they always came home. It's what they did.

Even David Williams…

Callum walked over to the shower, reached in and turned the wall nozzle on. He decided he could do without the rain-like spout pouring down on him. He stripped out of his damp clothes, and opened the bathroom door again, dropping them on the floor so Garrick could chuck them in the dryer. He went and leant his bare ass against the sink cabinet, waiting for the shower to heat up. Out the corner of his eye he noticed a small business card on the ground. He bent down to pick it up and have a closer look.

Niemand Plumbing Services.

The business card belonged to Johan. One of the guy's from Callum's former tightknit social group. He brushed the card with his thumb, like he were touching a memory. He was glad to have Garrick in his life. He was a great friend. Still, Callum couldn't help but miss those days where he, Tim and Johan would all meet up after work and go out for drinks, swapping bullshit stories and pointless yarns.

Good days...

Callum noticed that the room had misted with warm fog. The shower was ready. He put the card down and crossed the floor to the shower, stepping under the warm spray. He picked up a black shower gel bottle and squirted a dollop of blue liquid into his palm, lathering its zesty scent under his arms and between his legs.

He looked down at his dick, giving it a light tug of sympathy. "Sorry," he said to himself and his cock. Coming so close to getting laid made Callum realise how much he could do with getting his rocks off. Ten months was a long time to go without sex and the thought of Dawn's jiggly tits buried in his face was a hot prospect. He briefly contemplated jacking off, releasing some of his tension but he thought better of it. He should probably spare corrupting his mate's new shower with his jizz and just wait 'till he got home.

He usually relied on a photo of Misty he kept beside the bed to give him ammunition for his self-pleasuring. It was just a simple face shot but he would stare at it and imagine her luscious lips wrapped around his knob. Blow jobs hadn't been a frequent occurrence in their relationship. Misty tended to reserve them for birthdays and their anniversary. A sort of sexual treat. Still, just conjuring up memories of her naked body was enough to usually make him splurge his load into a dirty sock or t-shirt that he would then drop to the side of the bed.

Just as he lulled his head back under the water, he heard the door to the bathroom creak open.

"Whataya think of the shower?" Garrick said, walking in and closing the door.

"Yeah. It's pretty good. A little bit swanky."

"Well, I'm a swanky guy." Garrick sat down on the

edge of the bath which was directly across from the shower. *The see-through shower.*

Callum mumbled on a laugh. He started washing his crotch, using his hands to give himself some modesty.

"You don't have to cover it up, mate," Garrick said. "I have a cock of my own remember?"

Callum nodded, feeling foolish. He turned to his side, slowly removing his hands and continued rubbing his body down under the water.

"That fucking Sherry, man." Garrick sighed, resting his elbows on his knees. "I can't believe how close I got with her tonight."

"Umm, I think you got about as close as the earth is to the moon."

"Nar. Me and her had chemistry."

"If you say so," Callum said cheekily. He scrubbed his hands over his face and into his hair, clenching the blond strands. He found it amusing that Garrick thought he was close to getting laid tonight. The guy had been nowhere fucking close.

"Mark my words. Sherry will be back. She wants a piece of this," Garrick grabbed his cock through his trousers, giving it a firm grope.

Callum didn't bother trying to deflate his mate's delusion. He figured it wasn't fair to rub the guy's face in it. Garrick wasn't used to the taste of defeat, and tonight, if he liked it or not, he had been served a huge plateful.

Callum turned the water off and stepped out of the shower, grabbing his towel from the rail. He looked over at Garrick and asked, "Do you think my clothes will be dry enough now?"

Garrick went to stand up but hesitated. "Maybe now is a good time for you to start cleaning the lounge."

"Now?"

"You're naked and the lounge is right there," Garrick said, throwing out a devilish grin.

Callum laughed, snaking the towel between his legs. "Piss off." He looked over and saw Garrick watching him gently. "You're actually serious?"

"I am. The deal was if you lost then you had to clean my lounge... naked."

"You're taking the piss, right?" Callum grinned back at his friend.

Garrick shook his head solemnly. "A deal's a deal, buddy. A man should always stick to his word."

"So, you want me to stay like this... butt fucking naked and go out there and clean your mess up?"

Garrick nodded, smiling. "Yep. You lost remember?"

He stood still for several seconds, thinking out the logistics of what had been requested. "Fuck sake," Callum muttered under his breath. He knew this was Garrick's way at getting back at him for having received more attention from the girls.

"Don't be such a soft cock."

Callum hated being called that. "I'm not a soft cock."

"Then why are you backing out?"

"I'm not backing out." Callum sighed. "Just let me finish drying off and I'll come out and start cleaning, oh powerful master." He rolled his eyes.

"I prefer being called sir, but master will do too," Garrick replied in a bland tone. "I'll go pour myself another drink and let you get pumped up and ready to be my cleaning bitch."

"Har, har," Callum replied sarcastically. "At least put a fucking heater on 'cos I'll freeze my nuts off otherwise."

∞

Callum wandered into the lounge where he discovered the room to be toasty and warm. Garrick had turned the heat pump on high, settling the room to summer levels, safe from the bitter spring night outside. If he was gonna spend the next hour cleaning naked then he may as well be comfortable, Callum thought.

As comfortable as this can be.

It was fucking strange to be standing so exposed in

front of his mate without a stitch of clothing on. A part of Callum wanted to flip the bird and call Garrick a cunt for cashing in on a bet that Callum had assumed to be a joke. He knew better though. He couldn't let Garrick see his pissy resentment. That would only make Garrick feel like he had won some unspoken game. A game of nerve.

Garrick was sat at the dining room table, letting his eyes dance over Callum's nudity. He smirked. "I must say you're not the type of leggy blonde I usually have roaming around this place naked."

"Very funny, homo," Callum groaned. "So where do I start?"

Garrick took a sip of his drink before answering. He pointed to the piles of clothes strewn over the couch. "Probably best to start with folding the washing. You just might need to do a sniff test to make sure though." He simpered, laughing when he saw the look on Callum's face. "I'm joking. It's all clean, just fold it all up and chuck it in my room, would you?"

"Rightio, boss. What else did you want done?"

"Chuck the plates and glasses on the kitchen bench and just do a quick vacuum. After that I'd say you've paid your debt off."

Callum nodded. "Good to know." He was relieved that it was just folding the washing, clearing dishes and vacuuming the floor. He had thought Garrick would make him do a huge spring clean. Maybe he wasn't being a bitter prick as much as Callum had thought.

He went over to the pile of clothes on the couch, trying to fold them neatly. He was fucking useless with folding washing but he did his best. He couldn't believe how much washing there was. It appeared Garrick was treating the lounge and couch like a sort of bedroom dresser, too lazy to put his stuff away. When he took the clothes to Garrick's room, he placed them nicely at the foot of his unmade bed. As he went to leave the room, he very nearly stood on a milky-filled rubber.

Fucking gross, Garrick!

Apparently Callum's mate had gotten his end away and never bothered to discard of the evidence. Like fuck Callum was picking it up. That was a job for Garrick's manwhore fingers. Callum just hoped that by the next time Garrick had a girl come around he would have the good sense to get rid of it.

As instructed, Callum moved onto vacuuming the floor straight after finishing with the washing and clearing the dirty dishes from the lounge. He lugged the vacuum around, sucking up all sorts of dust and crap off the floor. As the vacuum's suction whirled with noise, Garrick seemed unfazed as he sat reading a magazine at the table, completely disinterested in Callum's cleaning frenzy.

Before he knew it, Callum was finished. "All done, mate." He wiped his brow, happy with his work.

Garrick rose from his chair and walked in. He looked around the room, nodding. "Well, well, well… if you ever get sick of being a chef then I think cleaning is the obvious career choice. Good job."

"Thank you."

"Take a seat, man, and I'll grab you a drink."

Callum went and nestled in on the couch, his bum and back jolted from the coolness of the leather.

Garrick returned and handed him a glass of rum and coke.

"Cheers," Callum said, taking a quick sip. He brought his feet up on the couch and tucked his knees under his chin.

Garrick sank to the floor in front of him, resting with his arms on his knees while holding his own glass of rum.

"Odd spot to take a seat," Callum said. "What's wrong with the couch?"

"Nothing. I just fancied sitting on the floor for a change." He stared around the clean room. "Cheers for doing the cleaning. I'm glad you followed through on the bet."

"Of course," Callum said. "I always keep my word. So remember that when I beat you next time." He wiggled his eyebrows playfully.

Garrick laughed. "That's fine by me. I never turn

down a challenge."

That was true. Garrick would never shy away from fulfilling a bet if he lost. Callum began wondering what he could do to get revenge if he won at the next game night. Something more embarrassing than cleaning naked. Before he could let his mind wander to sadistic payback, Garrick caught him off guard with a compliment.

"You've got nice legs for a dude." Garrick was unashamedly staring at Callum's sun-browned legs, nodding as he took in the sight.

Callum ran a hand up and down his shins, feeling his complimented area. "Thanks, man." He laughed. "Would be nice hearing that from a chick, but I'll take it."

"Everybody needs some ego fuel now and then," Garrick said, smiling up at him, sending Callum a confusing glare.

An awkward pause drifted between them.

"Are you feeling alright?" Callum asked light-heartedly. "You seem weird."

"Do I?"

"Yeah…" Callum tugged on his feet. "Have I done something to annoy you?"

Garrick cleared his throat. "No. Nothing like that."

"Then what is it?"

"Don't freak out, but I just wanna ask you to do something for me."

"Okaaay…" Callum curled his lip up. "What is it?"

"Can you open your legs?"

"Excuse me?"

"Your legs. Can you spread your legs apart for me?"

This was the strangest fucking request Callum had ever heard. He was about to laugh it off, assuming it was a joke, but Garrick's face appeared serious. *More than serious.* The guy wasn't joking, he really did want Callum to spread his legs.

Callum flashed Garrick a tight smile. He carefully put his drink down beside the couch then lowered his feet to the ground and spread his legs apart—giving his mate an eyeful.

Garrick flicked his eyes down to Callum's private parts, visually fondling his flaccid cock and squished balls.

"What are you doing?"

"Just looking," Garrick replied politely, not taking his eyes away from Callum's crotch. "Is that okay?"

"I spose. It's a free world." Callum left his feet planted on the carpet and his legs open wide for what felt like a dick inspection. He knew his body was fine but it didn't stop him feeling self-conscious from the way Garrick's dark eyes scrutinised his nakedness. If he was with any other guy in this situation he would probably be freaking out right now. But this was pussy-loving Garrick, not some perverted creep. Whatever this weird shit was that he was pulling, Callum could handle it. That didn't mean he wasn't grateful for what little booze he had coursing through his veins. Without it he didn't know if he'd feel quite so relaxed.

Garrick shuffled forward on the carpet, bringing himself closer. "I've always wondered what you look like naked."

"You saw me stark naked just thirty minutes ago in your shower."

Garrick stared up at him, his dark eyes glossed with a curious sheen. "I know, but not like this. Just right in front of me so I can look uninterrupted."

He must be more pissed than I thought. "You're sounding pretty queer tonight, dude."

Garrick opened his mouth taking a while to speak. "Haven't you ever wondered who has the biggest cock between us?"

"Can't say I have," Callum said, laughing.

"Bullshit," Garrick fired back.

"Why is that bullshit? Why would I spend a single second thinking about another man's cock?"

"Are you telling me that you've never been curious to know if your dick is bigger than mine? Not even once?"

"I've seen you walk around naked plenty of times, I don't need to wonder."

"Yeah, and I've seen you do a sneaky look to see."

Garrick grinned. "Which means I'm right."

"Okay. Maybe I'm guilty of sneaking a peek once or twice in the past just to compare. But that doesn't mean I sit at home fantasising about how big your sausage is."

"Yours is bigger by the way," Garrick said flatly, his eyes remained fixed on Callum's meat. "When flaccid at least."

"Thanks." Callum chuckled. "Finally, a game I can always win."

"Don't get too cocky, buddy. It's when it's hard that matters."

"True," Callum mumbled.

"Can I touch it?"

"My cock?"

Garrick nodded.

Callum swallowed a lump of nerves in his throat, his unease skyrocketing from the direction this was going. *He's pissed, just be cool,* Callum told himself. Garrick's charcoal eyes blazed with fire, releasing an energy that exuded undeniable control and bending him to his will. Callum took a deep breath and nodded. "If you like."

Garrick extended a hand, wrapping his firm fingers around Callum's dick and gave it a gentle squeeze.

The hair on Callum's neck began to bristle. He looked down with wide eyes, completely shocked at the sight of another male handling his tool. *This is seriously fucked up.*

Garrick loosened his grip, grazing his thumb over Callum's dick hole. "Nice," he whispered and casually retrieved his hand.

"Are you bisexual or something?" Callum asked, voice dropping an octave. He shuffled back into the couch, closing his legs up slightly.

"I'm definitely something."

"So you are bi?" Callum said more than asked. This felt like something Garrick should have shared long ago.

Garrick took a sip of his drink, taking his time to answer. "I wouldn't say I'm bi... just open minded."

"And what's open minded when it's at home?"

"It just means that I'm open to new experiences." He raised his eyebrows at Callum. "You only live once right?"

"Hmph." Callum ground his molars; unsure what to say. "Have you done stuff with guys before then?"

"Not exactly," Garrick answered. "I let a dude suck me off once and I've had a couple three-ways."

"You let a dude suck your cock!" Callum spluttered.

Garrick laughed. "It's not a big deal. I was horny and wanted someone to suck my cock and he was more than happy to oblige."

"Fuck," Callum muttered. "That's pretty bloody open minded."

"Are you telling me you've never done anything with another dude?" Garrick asked, sounding shocked.

"Never," Callum said, shaking his head.

Garrick squinted his eyes, scanning Callum's face for any hint of a lie. "Not even when you were a horny teen whacking off every five minutes?"

Callum thought about the question, throwing his mind back through the years to his pubescent days. "I didn't do anything with him, but when Tim used to stay at my place on weekends we'd beat off in the same room while watching porn." Callum shrugged as he looked down at Garrick. "Does that count?"

Garrick smirked. "I guess it sort of does."

"And I just let you touch my cock," Callum said. "So now I've got two same-sex experiences.

"True, mate." Garrick motioned his drink forward for a toast. "To exploring your sexuality."

Callum smiled, picked his glass back up and clinked it against Garrick's. "To exploring sexuality."

They both sculled back on their drinks and let the room fall silent for a moment. What had felt like a close call with awkwardness had gone. If anything, Callum felt strangely at ease to have shared such honest memories. He figured whatever Garrick had done in his past didn't make him any less straight. He was just *open minded* like he said.

Garrick was the one to break the quiet with a

question. "Would you be keen to try some exploring?"

Callum eyed him warily. "What sort of exploring are we talking here?"

Garrick lowered his voice to sexy levels and said, "Lay back on the couch and let me touch you a bit more." He tapped Callum's knee. "I wanna see how big your cock is *hard.*"

CHAPTER SIX

Ears buzzing with a hot rush of blood, Callum wasn't sure how he should react. *Garrick wants to touch me again... down there... he wants to see it hard.* This was all too fucking weird. He considered laughing and just saying he was too tired. If he declined the drunken offer politely then he could quickly finish his drink and leave. They could put it all down to the booze and forget about it tomorrow.

"You wanna?" Garrick asked softly.

Callum sat motionless before rubbing his face. "Wanna what exactly?"

Garrick's voice rose from the quiet level it had been. "Shit, I dunno, just have a fumble. A little play around."

A fumble? A play around? What did that even mean. The detail seemed purposely sparse. Callum took a hearty mouthful of his drink, feeling like he was stepping into a field of mines.

"Come on, man, when did you last get laid?" Garrick asked, trying to get him on side for whatever it was he was suggesting. He narrowed his eyes, prodding Callum to answer.

"It's been a while," he admitted.

"What's a while?"

Callum looked at the black pond of rum in his glass, blushing. "Ten months."

"Fucking hell, Callum! It'll fall off soon if you don't use the poor fella."

Callum laughed. "I hope not. I've grown quite fond of it after 28 years."

"Then all the more reason to let me help you out." Garrick nodded, smiling. "Give Mrs Palmer and her five daughters the night off."

Callum wondered if that meant Garrick was going to wank him off. Garrick's entire behaviour since they left the bar had been strange, he wondered how real this was. He quickly downed another mouthful of rum, emptying his glass. He sighed, and against his better judgement asked, "What are you offering?"

"Like I said I am keen to see how big your cock is when it's hard."

"But why? And that doesn't exactly answer my question."

Garrick chuckled. "I spose I am just keen to see who the bigger man is. Not that that shit matters, but it's just something I'm curious about." He pulled at his dark fringe, smiling. "And to answer your question, I am offering you a blowie." Garrick prodded the inside of his mouth, sticking his cheek out with his tongue, hammering home what he meant.

"A blow job?" Callum squawked. "You'll put my dick in your mouth?"

Garrick laughed. "Yes, Callum. I believe that is what a blow job means." His eyes lingered towards Callum's crotch.

"Fuck a duck," Callum muttered. "You're crazy, man."

"Are you telling me you don't like being sucked off?"

"No…" Callum hesitated. "I love my cock being sucked as much as the next guy, but my preference is the person sucking it has minge and tits."

"I bet you I can give you a better suck than any chick has."

"I thought your *exploring*," Callum raised his hands to insinuate inverted commas, "was just being sucked off by a guy—not the one sucking."

"I've honestly never sucked a guy off before," Garrick answered. "But I've had enough blow jobs in my life to know what makes it feel good. I know not to scrape with my teeth." His face grimaced like he had heard fingernails dragging down a blackboard.

"I-I don't know what to say." Callum took a breath, bouncing his leg.

"Don't freak out." Garrick touched his knee gently to stop his shaking. "I just thought it would be cool for us to do something special. Something just between us."

Callum looked down at his droopy dick then at Garrick's full lips. He scanned the room making sure curtains were pulled. He had just enough booze in him to drop his guard and entertain the thought. "But what would people say?"

"Nothing," Garrick said firmly. "Who else is here?" He looked around the room. "It's just you and me. No one else is here to see what we do or don't do."

Just politely say no and leave it at that. Callum went to reply, but the decline on the tip of his tongue dried up when he saw the look on his mate's face.

Garrick's lips ever so slightly pouted, looking like he was blowing the most gentle of pleading kisses. There was a carnal wanting simmering beneath those beautiful coal-dark eyes. It wasn't messy and unorganised like Dawn's flirt had been at the bar. It was controlled and pure—deep with meaning.

This was raw... passionate... sensing.

Callum hadn't been contemplated like that in so long. *Too fucking long.* He felt wanted. He felt craved. Maybe even loved.

Silencing the staunchly straight male voice in his head telling him he should run, Callum relented without saying a word. He put his empty glass down then lifted his feet up, twisting 'round and laying back on the couch, extending his body out like a patient waiting for an examination.

Garrick shuffled along the floor to the end of the couch, sitting at the end Callum's feet dangled over. He swivelled his thumb around the sole of Callum's bare foot, tickling him softly. "I can't wait to see you hard. I bet it's a huge monster."

Callum coughed up a laugh and said, "You'll be sorely disappointed if that's what you're expecting."

"You could never disappoint me, Callum. Never." Garrick smiled at him. "Are you sure you're cool with this?"

"If this is something you wanna do then yeah... I'm cool with it." Callum sighed. "Like you said. You only live once, right?" He closed his eyes, letting Garrick steer the journey of discovery.

Garrick slowly glided his strong hand up Callum's leg, grazing his fingers along the hairy terrain. "Seriously, buddy. You do have nice legs." He gripped hold of Callum's calf muscle, squeezing, before continuing higher.

Callum clenched his jaw as he felt Garrick's hand climb past his knee and dart to the inside of his thigh, challenging his sexuality every inch of the way.

Garrick's hand came to a smoothing stop just below Callum's balls. He delicately squeezed hold of the sac, giving his nuts a soft tug, rubbing his thumb over the freshly shaved texture. "You must have tidied up downstairs recently."

Callum nodded and croaked out, "Yes. Just the other day."

"Nice. They feel great." Garrick chuckled. "I bet they taste great too."

Callum let a trapped breath escape when he felt Garrick's tongue licking at his scrotum. His mouth fell open and his hands twitched. *Whoa!* He opened his eyes to see what was being done to him. Garrick's face bowed down servicing his ball sac as his hands kept rubbing inside Callum's thighs. "Oh, man..." His legs trembled the more Garrick lapped up his balls.

Garrick pulled his face up, big grin on his face. He kissed Callum's stomach, licking the golden trail of hair below his belly button. "Time to get this fucker hard." He dropped his face back down and took Callum's cock inside his stubbled mouth, sucking firmly.

Callum blinked, powerless to respond. *Fuck. This is bad. Really fucking bad.* He had to stop this going any further. But he couldn't. Even though the lips wrapped around his shaft belonged to another man—*my good fucking mate*—Callum just didn't have the strength to break away from his first blowjob in over two years.

He glanced down his body and saw Garrick's smoky

eyes looking back at him, pupils widening in heady lust.

He's enjoying this. How bloody queer is he? Callum felt his cock begin to stiffen. He desperately tried to hold in a gasp. His thickening did not go unnoticed.

Garrick groaned affirmatively and began to suck harder, making wild slurping noises. He reached up and tweaked Callum's nipple. With his other hand, he cupped Callum's balls, jiggling them around like he was feeling their weight before dipping a thick finger and began to rub the ridge of his taint.

Callum writhed, curling his toes and groaning loudly. Garrick knew where to touch. He knew the spots. And he was pinching, sucking, slurping, rubbing all the right fucking places. Callum was embarrassed by how fast he became fully erect; his cock aching from being so hard.

Garrick's effortless sucks became gagging mumbles as he tried to accommodate for the increase in size his mouth was feeding on. This didn't stop him from continuing to work both his hands like magic, fingers clawing at Callum's chest and midriff whilst fiddling with his tightening sac. Finally, he tore his mouth free from Callum's cock. "Looks like somebody's enjoying himself."

Callum panted, nodding. "You... you are fucking awesome at that."

Garrick tapped Callum's erection. "So this is what he looks like hard, aye?" He gave a smug look.

Callum blushed. "Yep. Just an ordinary cock. Nothing impressive."

Garrick stroked his length, sizing him up. "About six inches, yeah?"

"Six and a half."

Garrick laughed. "Sorry. Them half inches do matter." He kissed the tip gently. "Mmm. Someone has a bit of precum going on." He kissed it again, this time digging his tongue in the slit, tasting Callum's sex.

"I can't believe we're doing this," Callum said. He covered his face with his hands and groaned.

"Hey, hey," Garrick said, patting his leg. "Don't be

like that. We're just two mates having some fun. Nothing wrong with a bit of fun, is there?"

Callum peeled his hands away. "I Guess you're right."

"Of course I am right. I'm always right."

Callum smiled. He began to feel stupid being laid out naked, not doing anything. He swallowed. "Did you want me to do anything?"

"Did you want to do something for me?" He lowered his face again and bit Callum's flank, emitting a low growl.

"Umm... if you want me to?" Callum didn't feel like he had control of this interaction. Garrick was in the driving seat. It was up to him what they did. Callum didn't have a clue.

"If you wanna be a pal, then come down and join me on the floor and take my pants off for me." He scooted back away from the couch giving Callum room to join him.

Callum sat up and lumbered down off the couch, positioning himself in front of Garrick who sat with his legs apart and knees bent.

Garrick tapped one of his shoes with his hand, motioning for Callum to take them off for him.

Driven by a curiosity he had never known before, Callum didn't question the instruction. He wasted no time in yanking Garrick's shoes from his black sock-covered feet, casting them aside. Next, he leaned forward and fiddled with Garrick's belt, popping it open. With shaky fingers, he popped open the pants button and tugged on the cool, metal zipper.

Garrick ripped his top off and lay down, raising his ass off the floor.

Callum hooked his fingers over the waistband of the pants, dragging his mate's trousers all the way down, wrestling them free from his feet. Garrick's legs lay stretched out before him; muscular and strong, sprinkled with dark hair. *Great legs.* This wasn't a surprise. What was though, was the overly generous bulge tent-poling Garrick's blue boxer briefs.

"Are you hard?" Callum stupidly asked, knowing the

answer.

"I am." Garrick patted his bulge, smiling. "All thanks to you."

"But I haven't done anything yet."

"Maybe I only need to look at you to get turned on?"

"Really?"

"Yes, really. Why wouldn't I? You are a sexy bastard after all."

The praise was dizzying. It didn't matter that it came from a guy. It was coming from Garrick. Probably the best-looking dude in Tasman Heights.

Garrick promptly hoisted his underwear down his legs, flinging them across the floor, leaving himself wearing nothing but a pair of socks. He swung his legs apart, strategically placing them either side of Callum; enclosing him in a sex zone. He looked up with a goofy grin on his face. "Whataya think?" The way he said it reeked of arrogance, but he had every right to be.

Callum nodded, replying internally. *You're fucking perfect. Perfection with a cock.*

His mate was the proud owner of a big dick. Callum's wasn't even a close second in length or girth. The thick piece was probably only a whisker away from eight inches. It had the slightest of curves and pointed high with confidence.

"You can touch it if you want," Garrick said, scratching the crisp line of hair that plunged below his perfect navel.

Callum suppressed his remaining stubborn jitters and gingerly reached out, grabbing hold of his mate's stick. Smooth hotness filled his fingers, throbbing. He drew breath through his nose, urging himself to keep playing. He rubbed the pad of his thumb over a thick creeping vein, exploring the detail of the dick in his apprehensive grasp. He began to glide his furled fingers up and down, tugging harder, and harder.

Garrick grinned foolishly, his plump fuzzy balls bouncing in time with the hefty tugs. Suddenly, his hand flew up and closed over Callum's wrist. "Easy, buddy. Easy."

"Did I hurt you?"

"No. You just seem in a big rush."

"Sorry, I'm just a bit stressed out."

"Just relax, man. Nothing to be stressed about. It's just you and me. Two mates having some fun." He sat up and brushed the side of Callum's face, smiling.

The affectionate touch was sweet relief, like rain in the desert.

"How about you chill out and have a go at sucking me?"

Callum swallowed a tiny gasp. He looked down at Garrick's cock, towering above his untamed pubes. *He wants me to put that in my mouth?* So far, Callum had been the one receiving most of the pleasure, now it was his turn to gift some physical joy.

"Come on, man. I sucked yours." Garrick lay back down, resting his arms behind his head. An air of expectation firing from his sculpted body, giving an invisible slap to Callum's face.

Callum's pulse ticked in his throat. He inhaled, opening his mind as he prepared to close his lips around another man's cock for the first time in his life. In slow motion, his face dropped like a skydiver who forgot to open his parachute, crash-landing open-mouthed over Garrick's penis. His taste buds colliding with salty dick sweat.

Straight away, Garrick pulsed inside his mouth. He erupted with a loud groan, sounding like a guy who had been busting for a piss.

The strange feeling in his mouth wasn't what Callum had expected. Garrick's cock didn't taste good or bad. The musty sweat tasted mostly of... size? Callum wasn't sure what else to call it. All he knew was that his mouth was packed with a foreign fullness making him gag and slurp.

Garrick's moaning began to settle, he grabbed a tuft of Callum's hair, guiding his mouth, willing him to go lower.

Unsure the best way to suck a cock, Callum mimicked the tricks Garrick had done to him. He rubbed a finger along Garrick's prostate, massaging the ridge running from his balls to the bottom of his hairy crack.

Garrick's legs shook about, his mumbled moans echoing in the room as he flexed his fingers in Callum's hair.

Spurred on by the sexy noises, Callum dug his tongue into the groove of Garrick's dick slit, sending his mate's whole body into a rolling shiver. His tongue was instantly rewarded with a sexual sweetness—*precum!* Callum screamed the word in his mind, shocked and enthralled at the same time to have Garrick leaking ball juice in his mouth. The more he sucked and swivelled his tongue, the more trickled out.

Garrick pumped his hips, feeding Callum's mouth a steady supply of dick.

His jaw began to twinge, mildly aching from being rammed so fully with man-meat.

Suddenly, Garrick pulled Callum's mouth free. "So what's it like sucking my cock?" His lush lips split into a grin.

Callum sucked in a deep breath. "Different."

Garrick heaved his weight forward, sitting up. "Do you like it? My cock?"

"It's quite a big beast."

Garrick gripped hold of Callum's dick, giving it a hefty squeeze. "We now know what each other looks like hard."

Callum blushed, feeling small. "Yep. And we know yours is bigger."

Garrick looked down, comparing the size of their cocks. "Yeah, it is," he said bluntly.

"Don't rub it in."

Garrick kissed him on the forehead. "Sorry. I Didn't mean to sound like a *big dick*." He smiled and stared Callum in the eyes. "I like your cock though. It's sexy just like you... and it tastes great."

"Ha. Cheers," Callum said. He gazed into Garrick's brown eyes. He never knew how sexy they were... how dangerously captivating. He let his eyes wander, absorbing every detail of Garrick's handsome face. It was a sexy contradiction the way his facial features looked delicate and manly at the same time. "You're so fucking good-looking, Garrick."

"Ditto." He kissed Callum's forehead again.

Callum touched Garrick's arm, squeezing his bicep. As soon as he touched the taut skin, he realised this was something he had always wanted to do—feel his mate's strength.

Garrick strained his arm, flexing the muscle. He kissed it, grinning with pride.

The power of his friend's body was undeniable. These arms represented strength and power. A part of Callum wanted to know what it would feel like being hugged and circled by them. He imagined there would be no place safer than being wrapped up in these arms. He let his hand wander to the nest of hair on Garrick's chest, dragging his fingers through the virile feature, making coarse scratching noises. "This is so fucking weird," he whispered.

"A good weird I hope," Garrick said.

"Yeah… it's a good weird." He looked up and held Garrick's gaze. "Can I ask you something?"

"You can ask me anything you like."

"Can I kiss you?"

Garrick frowned, his lips cracking a broken smile.

"Sorry, sorry," Callum said. "I shouldn't have asked. Forget it." He laughed nervously, worried that he had overstepped a line.

"Of course you can kiss me, idiot." Garrick pressed his lips forward and slipped his tongue inside Callum's mouth.

Their tongues were like magnets, drawn together, swapping saliva.

The kiss was steamy.

And wet.

Hard and hungry.

Callum got lost in the moment, his urges unleashed like a caged animal tasting freedom for the first time. He leaned forward, pushing Garrick back 'till they tumbled wrapped together on the floor, resting on their sides. Even with the unforeseen fall their kiss didn't split. They kept their lips fused together, feeding groans into one another's mouths.

Garrick reached over, grabbing Callum's back and reeling him in so their stomachs were touching and their cocks locked like burning swords. He ran his hand up and down Callum's back, stroking seductively as his nails grazed the smooth skin.

Callum thought he would melt like butter in a pan. Garrick's chest hairs entwined with the few of Callum's own, creating a friction that was intensely sexual and undeniably male.

Finally, the need for air saw them ply their lips apart.

"Whoa," Callum panted. "You're a good kisser."

Garrick grinned back, dazzling Callum with his dimples. "I bet you say that to all the boys."

"Considering you're the only boy I've ever kissed, then yeah I do."

"Am I better than the girls you've kissed?"

Callum rolled his eyes to the side. "You'll need to kiss me again just so I can be sure."

Garrick didn't hesitate. He promptly placed his tongue back inside Callum's mouth for another sticky kiss. When he pulled back, he surprised Callum with a light nip to his bottom lip.

"So? How do I compare now you've had a second kiss?" Garrick asked.

Callum rolled his tongue up in his mouth, savouring the sweet flavour of rum left behind from Garrick's lips. He started laughing.

Garrick nudged him in the side playfully. "Oi, don't take the piss."

"No. It's not that." Callum began blushing and lowered his voice to a whisper, "You're probably the best kisser I've ever had."

"Yeah? Well that is fucking awesome to hear."

Callum's cheeks kept burning with shame from his confession.

"You're adorable when you're all embarrassed," Garrick said, pecking him on the cheek.

Callum shook his head in wonder. "I can't believe you

convinced me to try something like this."

"I should have been a salesman, right?"

"Yeah. You should have," Callum said. "But fuck, I'm glad you sold me this." He pulled Garrick in for a tight hug. "I didn't know I'd enjoy it so much."

"That's high praise for someone who hasn't even cum yet," Garrick joked.

Callum nodded. "Shall we jerk each other off?"

"I've got a better idea."

"You do?"

"Yup." Garrick nodded. "You should let me fuck you."

CHAPTER SEVEN

Callum felt his body jolt at the probing suggestion. "Whoa! I wasn't thinking we'd go that far."

"Come on, man. It'll be fun. More exploring. It'll be a first for both of us."

"I... I don't think I'm prepared to do that."

"You know I'd never do anything to hurt you." He rubbed Callum's knee. "You're my best mate."

Please don't say that.

"I know you wouldn't, but the whole idea of being fucked really freaks me out." He glared across at Garrick. "Seriously."

"Yeah. But I would go really gentle and slow." Garrick moved his hand higher up Callum's leg, fondling just below his balls. "It would be an honour to be let inside you in such a special way."

"It would?"

"Yeah, man. I would be the only guy you've ever let do that and it would be an awesome way to... I dunno... feel closer to you, I guess."

"But your cock is fucking massive."

Garrick laughed. "It isn't *that* massive. Besides, I have plenty of lube we can use to make it easier. Not to mention a fresh pack of condoms someone bought me tonight." He winked.

Callum now regret purchasing the bloody things. His mind wandered to David Williams. A person he had given plenty of shit to at school for allegedly doing some of the things Callum had done tonight. *Gay things.* He looked Garrick in the eyes. "This is something you really wanna do? You really want to fuck me?"

"Yes," Garrick answered. "I really want to fuck you."

He shot Callum a look that oozed sex appeal and sincerity. "Let me make love to you."

Love…

Callum felt chills fire up his spine. "I just…"

"Please," Garrick's voice pleaded. "It would be an honour."

"Fuck, your good at this."

"I'm being honest. It would be an honour." Garrick didn't falter in his sincerity. "I'll kiss you while I do it."

"Okay then," Callum said, hurling himself over the edge of curiosity.

Garrick gripped his thigh, giving an eager squeeze. "Really? You're sure?"

"Yes, I'm sure." Callum laughed. "You can fuck me." It felt strange saying it out loud but there was a thrilling perversion attached to it.

Garrick bounced to his feet. "Wait there, big boy." He gave Callum a kind smile and disappeared from the lounge. When he returned, he carried a small bottle of lube and the new packet of condoms in his hands. "I've got the goods."

Callum eyed the size of Garrick's thick manhood, he couldn't fathom that he was about to have it go inside him. He felt his asshole twitch.

"Are you sure this is a good idea?" Callum asked, having second thoughts.

"Why wouldn't it be?"

"Won't it make things weird between us?" Callum scratched his neck. "How will we act in the morning when we're sober?"

"We've already had each other's cock in our mouths." He looked down at Callum, giving him a reassuring gaze. "It'll be okay. I promise."

Callum sighed. "Yeah. Sorry. I'm just being a chicken shit."

Garrick dropped to his knees and rubbed Callum's leg. "Stop being a chicken shit then." He leant forward and kissed Callum on the lips, melting away the trepidation. "Now lay down and relax."

Callum did as he was told, lying down flat on his back. Icy anxiety avalanched through him as he heard the condom packet rip open. He lifted his head to see Garrick sliding the dull, yellow rubber down over his thick member. It looked fucking scary the way it shielded his shaft like a weapon, a weapon that was ready to go to battle inside Callum's asshole.

Garrick grabbed hold of Callum's feet, gently sliding his legs apart to sit between them. He grabbed hold of Callum's furry calves and rolled him upwards so his ankles dangled high in the air.

Callum squeezed his eyes shut, awaiting a painful impact, but what he was hit with was the weirdest pleasure he had ever felt. The warm, wet groove of Garrick's tongue licking the indent between his ass cheeks, tracing the inside of his crack and wetting the closed rim of his hole.

Callum gasped, his eyes widening. "What the fuck are you doing?"

Garrick popped his face above Callum's crotch, "Licking your ass out. What do you think I'm doing?"

"Is-is that a thing?"

Garrick laughed. "Yes, Vanilla Bradshaw. It's a thing alright." He dropped his face back down and returned to licking Callum out.

Callum writhed in pleasure at the feel of Garrick's tongue gliding so effortlessly, wetting the wispy hairs inside his crack. This was so fucking personal and an invasion of his personal space. His ass was his alone. No woman had ever done this to him. And yet here he was on his back, feet thrashing in the air as his mate's tongue feasted on his trembling hole. Callum leaked out hankering groans, letting Garrick know he wanted more of what was being done.

Garrick seemed happy to oblige, he planted a finger to Callum's entrance and gently—*so fucking gently*—prodded Callum's asshole before digging his tongue back down to his ass, smothering his hole with spit and firm tongue flicks. Garrick withdrew his tongue from its anus digging and licked down Callum's taint 'till he came to his balls and mouthed his sac, soaking it thoroughly.

Callum embarrassed himself when he cried out a vulnerable sigh, "Ohhh, yesssss."

Garrick sucked harder, stopping just before it became painful. He spat Callum's balls out and muttered a quiet laugh. "You sorta sounded like a chick just then."

"Sorry," Callum gasped.

"Don't be sorry. I'm glad you're enjoying it," Garrick said. "It means I am doing my job right." He patted Callum's ass cheeks then lowered him back to the floor. He reached across the floor for the lube bottle, picking it up and squirting a healthy dollop into the palm of his hand.

"Are you going to…" Callum started.

"Going to what?" Garrick replied cheekily.

"Fuck me now?" He looked up with cautious eyes.

Garrick nodded. "That's the plan, mate."

Callum's breathing became short and desperate. He didn't know what to do… so Garrick did it for him. His hand dived between Callum's legs, sliding the slippy lube around his asshole. Callum's body jolted in shock from the cool wetness being placed against his anal virginity. Garrick massaged the lube delicately around Callum's hole, slipping him calming glances.

Callum's heart pounded like a thousand horses galloping inside his chest. He brought on his own eclipse, closing his eyelids and allowing himself give in to the erotic touch of Garrick's hands. Touches that teased out a temptation he couldn't deny. He knew that pain would be coming but he welcomed it; he wanted Garrick inside him.

Garrick raised Callum's legs again, wrapping them around his hips and yanked Callum closer to his body. He pushed his dick down, positioning it against Callum's puckering asshole. He grazed it kindly against the tight surface quivering in anticipating fear. Garrick's voice penetrated Callum's ears, "Ready or not. Here I come." With the slightest of shoves the head of Garrick's cock plopped inside.

They gasped in unison.

Callum grimaced, tensing up immediately. He took a

deep breath trying to gauge that he actually had the tip of his mate's cock inside his ass.

As if Garrick could sense his painful headspin he placed a hand to Callum's chest, quietly hushing him. "You're okay. I'll go slow. I want you to enjoy this too."

Callum nodded back, relieved for Garrick's concern.

Garrick dragged his blunt nails down Callum's hairy thighs and pushed forward feeding another inch of hard prick inside the virgin hole.

Callum felt his anal walls expanding around the invading meat. He hissed out a breath of pain but quickly gritted his teeth. "Go slow, slow, slow..." his voice petering out.

"I will, don't worry, buddy." Garrick's hands kept rubbing and massaging. He pushed his slick rubbered cock deeper inside, claiming more and more of Callum's untouched places.

Callum's pucker wrapped around Garrick's mighty penis. He couldn't believe something so thick was tunnelling inside a hole so small. His ass was being put to the test but it was adapting, opening.

Blinking, flinching, Callum gasped.

Impact.

Garrick's hairy balls pressed against his ass.

The room fell silent and heavy in mood. Neither moved for a moment, just staring into the other's eyes. This was monumental. Two good mates, regular blokes, connecting in an unspeakable way. One's cock buried fully inside the ass of the other, sharing their existence in the most personal way possible.

Callum reached up, touching Garrick's face. Garrick smiled, kissing his palm. He dropped his fingers to Garrick's chest, catching his heartbeat in his hand. Callum was undeniably full—physically and emotionally, as his mate's cock throbbed inside him.

He has his cock fully in me! I am actually getting fucked by another guy!

Eyes bright, Garrick pulled his cock back and tipped

his hips forward against the friction of Callum's hole. He pulled back again, bucking forward again and again and again.

"Uh, uh, uh," Callum kept repeating. A haze clouded his brain. All he could focus on was the dense thumping spearing his centre, his ass gripping the curve of Garrick's boner, holding him in place.

"Callum—you—feel—" Garrick paused, biting his bottom lip. "So—Fucking—Good!" He lowered his head, capturing Callum's cock with his mouth.

Oh, man.

Callum gasped, losing all ability to make vocal sense, replacing words with pretty noises. His chest rippled with pleasure from being fucked and sucked at the same time. He had no idea Garrick was so flexible, but he was grateful for it. The harpooning of his hole was less pained with the sexy medicinal touch of his mate's wet lips wrapped around his dick.

Garrick took advantage of Callum's erotic writhing and began to fuck a bit harder, sliding in and out on side angles all designed to loosen Callum's reluctant rectum. He broke free from sucking Callum's dick and started planting kisses on Callum's stomach, maintaining his steady rhythm. He raked his fingers through Callum's trimmed pubes, stroking sensually as he continued kissing higher and higher.

You are too good at this.

He brushed his lips over Callum's left nipple, biting down gently and ravishing it with slick licks. The exploring continued with his tongue crawling to the centre of Callum's chest, licking the strands of blond hair growing there.

Callum held in a ticklish chuckle.

Garrick leant his weight forward, forcing Callum's legs even higher, hunching their bodies together in a slippery heat.

The folding up of his legs left Callum's ass even more vulnerable and Garrick struck the weakness by pushing his cock in with all his might. He was about to cry out but Garrick planted his lips to Callum's open mouth and caught his gasping sigh of hurt.

Their tongues tied together, merging, each sharing the

other's breath. He let go of the carpet and clawed at Garrick's broad back, holding him close so that their chests rubbed together. *This is fucking amazing.* He had never felt so at one with another person, nobody had ever left him feeling quite so vulnerable yet loved at the same time.

No longer scared of the pain impaling him—Callum craved it. He freed his ankles from Garrick's grip, squirming beneath him, adjusting his legs to wrap around Garrick's rump, pressing down, bringing him in hard.

Garrick's breath bled out, hot and heavy, spurred on by Callum's hunger. He ignited his hidden strength and unleased a series of furious shoves with his cock that went to the pit of Callum's core.

Garrick pulled his mouth away, slowing his fuck-flow. "Are you liking my cock?" he spat out in a breathy whisper.

"It's go-go-good," Callum replied with his head bobbing around.

"Fuck yeah." Garrick let out a low growl. "Your ass feels so good, man."

"Thank you."

Garrick drove his tongue into Callum's ear, tickling and wetting his eardrum before chewing on his earlobe. There wasn't a part on Callum's body his pal was afraid to touch or taste, every inch of flesh was included in the art of lovemaking. He grabbed hold of Callum's wrists, pinning them down on the floor above his head, locking him in place with no escape from what was being done to him.

Teeth slowly scraped the curve of his shoulder, followed by Garrick's tongue digging inside his armpit.

"That tickles," Callum heaved. He wriggled around, trying to break his hands free but Garrick pinned him down harder, continuing to lick the hair under his arm.

There was no use in fighting—Garrick was too strong.

Garrick kept slamming his pelvis into Callum's behind. His hairy balls slopped against Callum's ass cheeks, leaving Callum in no doubt as to who was in charge of this exchange. Garrick maintained a speedy pace, not showing any sign of slowing as he just kept fucking and fucking. Finally, he released his grip on Callum's hands and lifted his face up, shooting him a devious grin, spit dripping from the corners of his mouth.

Callum swept his eyes across his mate's hairy chest which was dripping rivers of perspiration, sweat glistening down his neck. He admired Garrick's dusky eyes and the dark stubble along his chiselled jawline. "You're so beautiful," Callum whispered without meaning to.

Garrick raised an eyebrow, smiling. Instead of replying, he raised Callum's foot, nipping it gently. He blew a warm breath over the skin he had just bit, and without warning, rammed his engorged cock in as deep as it could go.

Garrick's dick hit a spot Callum didn't even know existed, nudging him towards climax. "Oh... fuuuuck," he groaned loudly, nearly shouting out. His body shivered and a warm tingling swelled in his nuts, buzzing his cock. With a quivering lip he muttered, "I'm gonna cum,"

"You what?" Garrick blurted in surprise, still fucking his ass.

Callum threw his head back, squealing, completely lost in his orgasm—his cock just... shooting-shooting-shooting, gushing spurts of thick, creamy, white spunk. Wet dollops splattered against his stomach and chest like soggy bullets. His dick kept spurting, cum trickling down his shaft as he began emptying all of the passion that had been bottled up inside him for ten months. He lay with his head on the ground, Garrick still wedged inside him, breathing heavily from his unexpected release.

"That's like a porno load," Garrick said, amazed.

Callum nodded gently, wiping sweat from his brow with the heel of his hand. The room felt like it was spinning, sparks flickering at the edges of his vision.

"I can't believe you came from just being fucked." Garrick smiled, running a finger through the mess of sex draping Callum's torso. "Like... that's pretty intense."

"Yeah. I don't know what that was about."

"I do. You liked my cock so much I turned you queer."

"I'm not queer," Callum snapped back hastily.

"Really? So you don't have my big cock in your freshly-fucked ass right now?" The patronizing tone of his voice was infuriating and emasculating.

"And what does that say about you?"

"Not as much as it does about the one who just lost his lollies from being fucked."

Competitive arrogant Garrick was back. He probably never left—he had just been well-hidden behind the sex.

Callum wriggled backwards, trying to free his asshole from Garrick's cock. He grimaced as his mate's prick slithered out of him, his insides trying to return to their normal shape. He was about to roll over and stand up but Garrick placed a hand to his knee, stopping him.

"I'm not finished with you yet," Garrick said.

"Huh?"

"I need to cum. You don't get to go just cos you lost ya load in record time."

"It's hardly record time," Callum groaned.

"Okay. But you still gotta wait for me." Garrick pulled the condom off his cock and flung it across the lounge where it landed beside the coffee table in a light slurp. He stood up, leering down at Callum on the floor. "Don't worry I won't take long, mate." Garrick lowered himself down, kneeling on the floor beside Callum's chest. He began stroking his dick, working his fingers along his solid, fleshy length. His face screwed up with concentration as he began to grunt from the ferocious tossing. Finally, a grunt louder than the rest exploded from his lips and his cock swelled, shooting spunk out his slit, hitting Callum's chest and face.

The warm mess dripped down Callum's cheek down to his lips and chin. "You wanna try watching where you shoot ya gun," he joked, wiping his sticky face.

"Sorry." Garrick giggled, catching his breath. "Thought maybe you'd wanna try tasting it."

"I think I'll pass on that one."

"Maybe next time I'll just shoot in your mouth and make you swallow it all."

"What do you mean next time?" Callum croaked.

"The next time I beat you on game night." Garrick nodded. "Now I know I can play you for more than just cash."

Callum blinked, confused.

"I'm joking, buddy." Garrick leaned in and brushed their lips together. "Thank you for tonight."

"You're welcome."

Garrick slapped his shoulder. "Right I'll go grab us a towel, then I think we should call it a night." He stood up, arched and stretched his back.

What?

Like that, the moment was gone. Their deed swept under a rug.

Garrick walked away, leaving Callum sat naked on the floor, covered in cum and feeling like a lonely sin.

CHAPTER EIGHT

The next day was weird. A strange guilt plagued Callum's mind as if he had somehow betrayed his sexuality. All day at work he could feel Garrick's intimacy clinging to his body. The dark-haired lothario hadn't left any marks and the cum had been washed off thoroughly but Garrick's sexual effort lingered around the tenderness of Callum's battered hole.

He kept himself busy cooking in the kitchen, leaving the girls to work the front of house while Nicky cleaned up the stock room. He just wanted to be alone. Each time someone laid eyes on him, he worried that maybe they could tell what he had done last night. That they could tell he no longer owned a virgin ass. Not only had he taken a cock up there, he had taken a bloody big one. He knew this fear was absurd but what him and Garrick had done was absurd.

How the fuck did we end up even doing it in the first place?

Callum knew it was Garrick who had been the one to steer the harmless bet into sexual territory, but why had he allowed him to take it there? All he had to do was say no— but he hadn't. Was it because it had been so long since he last got laid? Were his blue balls that overdue for a proper empty that he had become so desperate and horny to actually surrender his ass?

The strangest part for him was how he had managed to cum from being fucked. The way Garrick's cock triggered something deep inside him posed questions. *Why'd I get off so much.* Sure, he could have hit a g spot. In fact, that was highly likely… but it didn't explain the rest.

The rest being how blinded Callum had been by Garrick's beauty as their bodies had become one. The lovers gaze they shared had been mesmerising, utterly captivating.

Each time Callum thought of it, he felt a flush of red blush his cheeks.

"Boss. I'm all done with the chiller room."

Callum turned around from the seafood platter he was preparing and saw Nicky waiting for his next order. He nodded and said to his employee, "Good stuff. I didn't think you'd be done 'till after lunch."

"It wasn't too hard. It was pretty easy actually." Nicky's face gave a panicked look. "Not that I didn't do it properly. I promise it's all tidied how you want."

Callum laughed. "Settle down, Nicky. I trust that you did the job well. You're my star employee after all." He smiled at his young worker. "Don't tell the girls though. They may get a bit jealous."

Nicky grinned, scuffing his sneakers on the kitchen floor.

"Did you wanna head home early?" Callum asked, hoping he could be alone in the kitchen today. But he knew what Nicky's answer would be.

"I'm okay, boss. Unless you want me to sign off early?"

Callum drew a breath about to say *yes* that is what he wanted. But he knew they may get busy for lunch and Nicky's help with the dishes would be needed. Besides, Julie would get pissed if he started making a habit of sending Nicky home early and cutting down his hours and therefore his pay.

"I forgot to order carrots with today's delivery. Grab twenty from the till and go down to the supermarket and fetch a dozen for me, will you?"

"Sure thing, boss."

"You don't have to rush. Consider it break time. Just be back before 11.30."

"Okay, boss. I'll go home and have a quick coffee with Dad and Julie then come back." Nicky smiled and walked out front to the till.

Callum grinned to himself knowing that Julie would be less than impressed to see her step son come home unexpectedly on a Saturday morning. Hiring Nicky wasn't just to help the boy out with a part-time job to learn new skills and earn some cash, it was to gift Julie and Graham Saturdays to be alone as a couple. Father and son were not aware of this. It had been a secret part of Julie's plan when she had asked Callum if he had a spare job going.

Julie wasn't horrible to Nicky, she was more than nice to the boy, but she had not been over the moon to have him come live with her and Graham. She was only 28 and Callum sympathised with her playing the role of stepparent to a full-grown teenager. When she began dating Graham she knew he had a son who would visit on school holidays and the occasional weekend but she had never imagined that Nicky would move in with them.

Nicky's arrival had been unexpected to say the least. Three months earlier Marissa—Nicky's mother—had rung Graham up out of the blue, crying, saying that Nicky was a handful she just couldn't deal with any more. She insisted he was just an out-of-control-teen who wasn't listening to a single thing he was told to do and getting up to mischief at school and had fallen in with a bad crowd.

Callum found this odd considering how wonderfully diligent the lad had been at work. He wondered if maybe the mother was crazy like Julie and Graham insisted she was. Graham had been split from Marissa for two years before he moved up to Tasman Heights and met Julie, but that didn't stop the former Mrs Cunningham getting upset about him moving on with a younger woman. Callum wondered if perhaps Marissa had thrown the best spanner in the works she could...her son. Julie now had to share Graham with his son every day and night of the week, testing her patience and maturity.

"Callum," said a girl's voice.

He spun round and saw Jess—one of his waitresses—coming in to the kitchen. "Yeah?"

"There's a woman here to see you."

"Who is it?" Callum asked.

"I don't know, sorry." Jess smiled. "But she's very pretty."

He frowned, cocking his head to the side to peek out the front. It was Sherry.

"Is she a new girlfriend?" Jess asked in a frilly voice.

"Ha. No, I'm afraid she's not." He smiled. "Can you take this out for me, please?" He quickly plated up the seafood basket and motioned for Jess to take the meal. "Thanks Jess."

Callum wiped his hands down his front and took his apron off. He moseyed through to the café front to go speak with Sherry. "You tracked me down, I see."

"It wasn't too hard to do," Sherry said. "Everyone in this town knows everyone."

"This is true." Callum smiled. "And who do I know that passed on my secret location to you."

"Callum, darling, I work with your sister and your bestest buddy in the world, so you have no secrets."

Trust me I do now.

Callum laughed, faking a jovial mood. He looked around at the quiet café. Only the table that had ordered the seafood basket was present. "Did you want to have a coffee?"

Sherry squinted her eyes. "Oh no. Nothing for me I just wanted to pop in and apologise for last night."

"Apologise?" Callum frowned. "What for?"

Sherry giggled as she stroked a hand through her long red hair. "Dawn and I came on a bit strong with you last night and I wanted to apologise if we made you feel uncomfortable at all."

"Umm, I can assure you I would never be made feel uncomfortable by two beautiful women flirting with me." As soon as he said it he felt sleazy.

"I totally agree with you on that point," she returned.

"So what is the problem?"

"Me and Dawn may have been a tad guilty of leading you on a little bit." She cringed. "Like a lot."

Callum's ego instantly took a dent. *Typical. It is Garrick they both like.* "Oh…"

"Not that you aren't a terribly handsome man." Sherry smiled. "Because you most definitely are."

Callum scratched his head, puzzled by her statement. "Sorry but you've got me really confused."

"Mandy isn't just visiting for a holiday. She lives with me. We are actually together."

Callum blinked. "You what?"

"We're partners, Callum. We're gay."

"Crikey," he blurted a little too loudly.

"I'm guessing you weren't expecting that."

"Nope. Definitely wasn't expecting that." Callum shook his head. "Then why were you both over me like… like shit to a blanket?"

Sherry laughed. "Gee, you really have a wonderful way with words, don't you?"

"I try." He chewed on his lip, trying to grasp what he had been told. "So if you and Dawn are a couple why would you be out on a double date with me and Garrick?"

"Well…" Sherry took a breath. "When I started work at the Council the girls warned me about a certain heartthrob who likes to make a point out of sleeping with every new employee with tits." She narrowed her eyes. "And I figured rather than let Mr Masters down gently I thought it might be fun to teach him a wee lesson and have him second guess his charms."

Callum cracked a smile. Finally, Garrick's manwhore ways were catching up with him. Sherry's plan was wickedly cheeky. "I think that is quite possibly the most awesome plan I have ever heard."

"You think?" Sherry frowned. "You don't think it is too mean?"

"Nope. Not at all. It'll do Garrick some good to learn what it is like to be a mere mortal."

"Yes. Based on some of the stories I have been told that is what I figured. Also, I hope it means he might buck up his ideas in future before hitting on a poor girl the moment she walks into the office."

"You can but hope."

"Anyway, that is why we both came on to you a little strong. We wanted to make him sweat in his boots a bit and

79

think that his best friend was the only one we were interested in."

Callum's pride was a little less wounded now but it didn't change the fact he probably wouldn't be Mandy or Sherry's first pick if they were attracted to men. "Good to be up to speed with the plan," he said.

Sherry nodded and looked around the café. "So the café is yours? Or are you the chef here?"

"Both. I used to work at Mokoia Resort up the coast as a Sous Chef and then four years ago Mum and Dad helped set me up in here so I could be my own boss."

"Very nice parents you have."

"Yeah they're awesome. But hey, I'm an awesome son too."

"Are you now?"

"Of course. I still turn up for family dinners every Sunday night without fail."

"Is that you being a good son or just because you miss your mum's cooking?"

"Both." Callum laughed. "It is quite nice to have someone cook me a meal for a change."

"For a change," Sherry repeated. "I don't suppose you do catering after hours, do you?"

"Sometimes. Not often but I have been known to try and expand the empire."

"How would you feel about doing a small function for me next weekend? It's only for about fifteen people. Nothing major."

"Really?"

"It's Mandy's thirtieth birthday and it would be nice to serve up some decent food for our guests rather than me trying to put together some ghastly looking antipasto."

"Sure. If you tell me what you are after then I can certainly sort that all out for you."

"Brilliant." Sherry rummaged through her handbag and dug out her business card. "Give me a call at work on Monday. I just need to finalise the numbers."

"Will do."

"And maybe you would like to stay and join us for the birthday festivities... tell Garrick that you have a hot date with both of us."

Callum snorted, holding in a laugh. "He would fucking kill me."

"Well, the offer is there. Try not to tell him just yet about the little game. I am looking forward to seeing him sulk at work on Monday. But I promise to end it before it gets too mean... just as soon as he looks like he has learned his lesson."

"Okay. My lips are sealed." Callum pretended to zip his mouth shut.

"Don't let the secret burn your lips too much," Sherry smiled and waved goodbye.

Callum blushed. He knew secrets could burn more than just your lips. They burned asshole's too.

CHAPTER NINE

The rest of the day at work crawled along slowly. It was a relief to finally get home and have a shower to wash the stench of the kitchen from his body. Callum ended up sitting on the couch in the lounge, wondering if he should go visit Julie for something to do. Normally, he would go 'round and see Garrick after work, especially on a Saturday night, but something was holding him back. That something being the fact Garrick had stuck his dick in his ass.

How the fuck did we wind up doing that?

This question had continued to rattle around in Callum's head all day. He had never swung that way before. *Never!* Before he met Garrick, he hadn't been the most adventurous of people. Sex to Callum was something special that you shared with someone you loved. Garrick of course had shown him that love was not needed to get your rocks off.

Since Misty left him, Callum had slept with a grand total of eight women. Most were from the first few months of his friendship with Garrick when his mate's influence was at its most powerful. At first, Callum had found the messy one night stands a source of fun and a great way to get over Misty's abandonment, but it didn't take long for him to realise that such a lifestyle wasn't for him. He cared who he shared himself with. He didn't want to be like Garrick who treated his cock like a ride at Disney World.

His mother had tried setting him up with friend's daughters on more than one occasion but nothing ever came from it. Callum argued that he was just too busy to settle down. Yes, he was busy but that wasn't the real reason for his reluctance. He was waiting for Misty.

He missed being part of a couple though, and he

82

definitely missed the sex, but if sex came with feelings then it ran too greater risk, he thought. And he couldn't risk being hurt again or replacing Misty who was definitely coming back to him one day.

Whilst Callum was hesitant to flick his body around for casual sex, last night hadn't felt casual. He wondered if the difference was that he knew Garrick. This wasn't some stranger he had met at a bar. Garrick was a good friend... they already had a connection.

Callum stretched out and lay down on the couch. He shut his eyes, remembering the details of the night before. It was so fresh in his mind, the memory permanently inked like a tattoo. He swore he could still smell Garrick's musty scent on his skin despite having two showers since their naked sweaty bodies had rubbed together. He wasn't sure if it was real or imagined but his hole still felt slightly ajar from Garrick's prick bursting him open.

His cock suddenly twitched and his eyes peeled open.

A chill swept over him. His dick was reacting to the replay of fucking in his mind. He looked around the room as if he were worried an imaginary housemate might walk in and know what he was thinking about.

He took a deep breath and closed his eyes again, giving himself permission to think about his first time with a man. And not just any man but a man so good-looking it hurt. He slowly slipped a hand under the waist band of his shorts, grabbing hold of his dick. He seized it between his fingers and began tugging on himself.

He imagined Garrick here on the couch with him, touching his body—touching him the way he had last night. No one had ever explored Callum quite like that. Garrick's hands were experienced for sure and he had used them to great effect. The way his fingers had pressed into his skin with deftly manoeuvres, rubbing up and down like they wanted to know more about Callum, not just physically but emotionally too.

"You made love to me," Callum whispered.

He raised his butt off the couch and tore his

interfering pants down to his knees. Callum played with his smooth balls, jostling them in his palm. He dropped a finger to his crack, grazing over the same wispy hairs Garrick's tongue had saturated. He circled slowly around his tenderised asshole, a place that Garrick had entered, claiming it as his own.

He pulled his hand back, sucking on his index finger and put it back down to his hole, gently pushing inside of himself. It felt weird doing this to his own ass. His finger was much smaller than his mates cock but somehow Garrick's sizable manhood seemed a better fit. Callum began pushing in and out, doing his best to replicate the feeling of being fucked. His dick burned with a hotness, thickening fast, and soon he was fully erect and panting as he finger-fucked his own hole.

Callum knew he was getting close to cumming, he was about to slip a second finger inside himself and go for gold but the sound of his phone blaring in his pants pocket stopped him.

"Fucks sake," he muttered, annoyed at his phone's bad timing. He reached down, fishing it out of his pocket and saw that it was a message from Garrick. His heart squeezed.

Fancy a game of cards? Come see me.

Callum bit down on his lip. He knew that if he went there now he would want them to try what they had done last night again. But was that a good idea? What if Garrick didn't want to try that again? *Garrick did say you only live once.* With a shaky hand Callum sent back a reply, giving into his temptation.

Okay. I'll be round soon.

∞

By the time he got to Garrick's the sky was beginning to darken. He hadn't got there as soon as he had planned because stupidly he fussed over what to wear. Usually he would rock on up to Garrick's not giving a shit what he wore. Not tonight. He had picked out his nicest jeans and put on a nice collared shirt. To top his dashing look off he had sprayed a light spritz of cologne on his writs and dabbed some behind his ears, wanting to make sure he looked and smelled sexy for his mate.

Immediately he regretted the effort he went to when Garrick answered the door in gym shorts and a manky singlet.

"Hey, buddy," Garrick said, eyeing Callum's fancy appearance. "I said come play cards, not take me out for dinner."

"Sorry, I uh…" the words dried up on Callum's tongue.

"I'm only joking, man. Come in."

Callum followed his friend inside and they went upstairs to the lounge. He sat down on one of the sofas, rubbing his sweaty palms down the legs of his jeans. "Place looks tidy," he said without thinking.

"That's 'cos you cleaned it, doofus." Garrick chuckled. "Seriously though, you did a primo job. Better than the last cleaner and I didn't even have to pay you."

"My services come cheap." Callum fought off the need to cringe. *Why did I just say that?*

"Apparently so." Garrick smiled, ignoring any accidental sexual connotations. "Anyway. What do you fancy to drink? Vodka? Rum? Sambuca? Beer?" The list could have gone on. Garrick's liquor cabinet and fridge was like the guy's sex life—never short on variety.

"Anything. You choose."

"Okie dokie. Two Smirnoff Black's coming right up then." Garrick disappeared to the kitchen before returning with two clanging bottles, handing one over to Callum.

"Cheers." Callum took a swig on the drink, hoping the booze could help calm the nerves bubbling in his veins.

Garrick went and took a seat across from him. He sat back in the couch confidently, spreading his legs wide. Callum found his eyes hone in on his mate's crotch, burning through the material. It was strange to think he now knew exactly what lay under there, how beautiful and big the dick was that lurked beneath the surface of Garrick's shorts.

So now I think cocks are beautiful... I am definitely losing it.

"Are you alright," Garrick asked, picking up on the nervous energy.

"Yeah, man. I'm fine." Callum forced a smile. "Just a bit tired. All work no play."

As soon as he said it he worried that Garrick would hit back at him about how they had played together last night. But he didn't.

"I know the feeling." Garrick pursed his lips around the bottle of vodka in his hand, gulping back a hearty mouthful. "Busy day, was it?" he unashamedly scratched at his groin, the outline of his balls becoming visible with the jiggling movement.

"It was dead in the morning but picked up once lunch time hit."

"You'll be glad when summer arrives and the tourists hit town."

"I reckon." Callum would be grateful. Summers was when he made his money. He barely stayed open through the quieter months and now with Spring nearly over, him and his wallet would be grateful for the upturn.

As they sat drinking together and talking shit, Callum slowly found himself reverting to a more comfortable state, almost forgetting what it was that had transpired between them less than 24 hours earlier. The evening cruised along like nothing had changed. Callum found himself grateful for this. Maybe the sexual fantasy he had earlier whilst on the couch at home was just his tired mind playing tricks on him.

Callum enjoyed their talking shit. They could literally speak about anything. Every visit he found himself sharing more about his past with Garrick who always sat with an intrigued look on his face, keen to learn more.

Tonight was no different with Callum telling Garrick about the time he was twelve and how he had seen a ghost in his grandmother's house. "Honestly, I nearly shit myself." Callum said. "It was my Great Aunt Candice walking through the hallway and she disappeared into my grandmother's bedroom."

"Like just disappeared?" Garrick asked, sitting on the edge of his seat.

"Yep. I walked down calling out to her but when I walked into the room she wasn't there."

"Maybe she jumped out the window to get away from you," Garrick teased.

"No." Callum's face turned serious. "An hour later my grandmother got a phone call to say that Aunt Candice had passed away at the retirement home she lived in... in Sydney."

Garrick shivered. "Brrr, that is a bit freaky."

"Yep. Bit spooky."

"So you believe in ghosts?"

Callum nodded. "I guess so." He looked at Garrick. "What about you?"

"I believe in anything 'till someone proves otherwise. I think it's important to be open to other's beliefs... you never know when they might become your own."

"Such a guru."

"That's me, buddy." Garrick got to his feet. "I think it's time you and me start playing some cards, don't you?"

"Sure." Callum followed his mate into the dining room where they sat across from each other at the table. "So what are we playing?"

"Poker?"

"Sweet. You deal then." Callum guzzled back on his drink. His third of the evening.

Garrick shuffled the deck speedily, making it look easy. He dished the cards out and hummed happily, letting Callum think he had a good hand. This Callum had learned was Garrick bluffing. But then he bluffed so much you never knew if the bluff was actually the truth.

Callum fanned his cards out, eyeing his hand. It wasn't great. He smiled anyway.

"I know you have a shit hand, Callum," Garrick blurted.

"How? I haven't said a bloody word."

"I know, but your lip curls up to the side too much

when you're faking."

"It does?" Callum laughed. "Remind me to never lie to you."

"Yep. Don't even try it." Garrick's eyes were focused on his own cards. "I will always know if you do."

"So what's on the table tonight?" Callum asked.

"If I am not mistaken, I think just a pack of cards and our drinks."

"No, dork. I mean what's the winner get?"

"I have fifty in my wallet. What are you putting up?"

"I don't have fifty. I never have fifty these days." Callum began to feel stupid. He hadn't brought cash with him for foolish horny reasons. He began to blush. "I could tell you a really good joke as a prize?"

"I'm more likely to see your Great Aunt Candice's ghost than you ever tell a funny joke."

"Cheeky sod." Callum laughed. "I'm telling you now the joke would be a good one."

Garrick smiled, looking across the table, holding Callum's gaze. "I think I can come up with a better prize if I had to."

"Can you?"

"I sure can." Garrick shot back a devilish grin. "Best of five rounds wins."

"You're on, Mr Masters."

∞

Garrick normally won most games of cards they played, but tonight Callum was on a roll. He won the first two rounds with ease and was painfully close on the next two. On the last round, he looked at his hand; he was in the winner's seat. He knew it. It was going to be a rare occasion to taste victory against Garrick. Callum began to get excited thinking about how the fifty bucks would help him.

Then his stomach knotted.

He discretely eyed Garrick's strong arms, wondering if he would get another chance to be wrapped up in them again.

His groin flared with desire. *If I win I could make him come clean my house naked.* The saucy image was titillating but Callum suspected Garrick would just insist he take the money and that would be fucking embarrassing trying to turn down fifty bucks in exchange to perve at Garrick's cock.

Not once had Garrick mentioned last night and what they had done together. Callum had wanted to bring it up, just to clear the air but it didn't feel right. If it was going to be discussed then it felt like Garrick should be the one raising the subject. He had started it. He had been the one who controlled the moment and in a way, was the owner of the deed and whether they brought it up or not.

This made Callum realise that if he were to have anything sexual happen with Garrick again, he would have to lose. He would have to take a chance on defeat to see what sort of prize Garrick wanted.

"Okay, mate. Ready to weep?" Garrick grinned across at him. He slammed his cards down on the table with premature glee. "Full house! And I ain't talking about the Olsen Twins." He placed down three jacks and two eights.

Callum looked down at his own hand—three Queens and two tens. He was about to cry out in victory but stopped himself. Did he want the money or did he want the chance to explore Garrick's passion again? It was all so confusing. He dillydallied.

"Hurry up, Bradshaw. What do you have?"

Callum made a split-second decision. "Fucking hell. Just when I thought you were gonna taste defeat." He laughed and threw his cards down, quickly burying them under the deck.

"What did you get?"

"Sweet fuck all," Callum lied.

Garrick narrowed his eyes. "Really?"

"Yep. Nothing but shit."

"Don't feel too bad. At least your consistent… even if it is at losing."

Callum joined in with the laughter. "True that. Well, I'll just go take a slash and when I get back you can tell me what my punishment is." He got up from the table and made his way to the bathroom. He planted his feet apart in front of the toilet and fiddled with his zip, unleashing his cock and sighed in relief as he emptied his bladder. Callum couldn't stop smiling, anxiously anticipating the punishment awaiting him. *Probably more cleaning.* He washed his hands and patted some water on his face to try and cool himself down.

He wasn't excited about the prospect of cleaning again but he knew he would be fast about it just so he could get the rest of his *punishment.* The punishment that wasn't a punishment if it meant Garrick would touch and love him like he had last night. He wiped his face dry, removing the giddy smile on his lips and returned to the dining room where he saw Garrick putting away the cards.

"So, mate. What's the verdict? Cleaning again?" Callum asked casually, trying to remove any hint of sexual nature to his voice.

"Nar, mate. You did such a good job last night that the place doesn't need to be tidied for a bit."

"Okay." Callum nibbled on his lip. He looked at Garrick's toned hairy legs, keen to feel them. "Nothing else I can do for you?"

Garrick harrumphed and grunted, "I'll have a think about it."

Callum felt his mood dip. Apparently, Garrick had no intention of cashing in his win in exchange for sex.

"What are you doing Tuesday night?" Garrick asked.

"Probably lazing about at home. Why's that?"

"The rugby's on that night. All Blacks versus Spring Boks."

"True." Callum wasn't much of a Kiwi when it came to rugby. He could take it or leave it. "Are you gonna be watching the game?"

"For the ridiculous price I pay to have the sports channel, I intend to watch every one of the big matches." Garrick laughed. "You should come watch it with me. You can pay me back then."

"Okay. I guess I can grab fifty from the till if the

takings are good that day."

"Keep the fifty. You need it more than me." It sounded degrading but it was true. Garrick squinted his eyes. "I think I might have something else in mind."

"Like what?" Callum asked, trying not to sound too keen.

"If you want to find out then you'll have to come 'round Tuesday, won't you?" Garrick's handsome face gave nothing away. "It's nice to have some surprises."

CHAPTER TEN

Tuesday morning was chilly and the cold gnawed at Callum's bones as he toddled along to work. He only lived a ten-minute walk from the café so he made sure he saved his gas and walked every shift. The mornings were his favourite. The town truly was a sleepy village at this hour—seven a.m.—and he loved seeing the ocean mist rolling in over the sheltered harbour.

He was grateful to have been born and raised in such a beautiful part of the country. As a teenager he loathed it, wishing he could move to Auckland and have a city life, but the older he got the more he came to appreciate why his parents never wanted to leave.

Even in recent years with more and more people moving north to buy a slice of this paradise, Tasman Heights still maintained its quaint charm. As sad as he would be to see the village lose its small size, Callum secretly wished it would grow faster to help keep his business stay afloat. Summer couldn't come fast enough.

After Misty had left him, and he had to pay her out her half of the house, Callum was in debt up to his eyeballs. No longer could he afford to employ another chef to give him Sundays off. He worked every day other than during the current off season where he wouldn't open on Mondays. This one day off was a blessing. If he didn't have it, he was sure he would fall apart from the hard work. He knew that come summer he would be losing this wonderful day off but it would be worth it just to pay off the bank loan and strained credit cards faster.

It was never meant to be like this. Misty and him were supposed to run the business together. Misty was a whizz with money. She could take a dollar and stretch it to twenty.

Her involvement was the only reason his parents had forked out such a generous deposit to get them started. Now they probably regretted ever doing so, knowing that Callum was left in charge. He may have been the sensible twin compared to reckless Julie, but he couldn't manage money. It just seemed to disappear when he touched it. Lost to random splurges on clothes, booze or anything shiny.

Fucking money! Callum loved it as much as he hated it. A necessary evil. Within a year of Misty leaving he found himself in trouble. However, he hadn't faltered yet. He was still treading above the water... just. The truth was his passion for the business had gone. His passion for food had gone. If mood affected taste of meals then everything he served up would be big balls of bitterly sour shit.

He probably could have sold the business to some out-of-towner looking for an investment in the area. It wouldn't give him much profit but it would probably clear his debt. But he refused to do this. By keeping the café open he was proving a point—that he was capable of running things on his own. He was a real man. Not the little boy Misty accused him of. And when she came back, then she would see he was more than capable of being what she needed.

Callum had been awoken not by his alarm clock but by the dream that haunted him. It was the same dream he had had ever since Misty had left him and it had become more frequent when his money problems began.

It always started the same. Beautiful and peaceful. He would find himself sitting atop a humungous tree, so tall it was like a skyscraper. In the distance he could see mountains, streams and the canopy of the forest below him. From up above he felt like a king, the ruler of a beautiful land. Unlike real life, things were good here. Everything felt right and he had a place in this world. No hurt. No lonely. Just peace. *Happiness.*

But then it would change...

The dream got dark. The skies would grey over and crashing blows of thunder would roll in. He would begin to smell smoke and the soles of his feet tingled with a niggly

Zane Menzy

heat. He would finally look down and see smoke clawing its way up, a fury of gnashing yellow flames racing towards him, wanting to swallow him like a monster.

It was absolutely terrifying. He had nowhere to escape. He couldn't fly in this dream. He had no wings or magical powers to extinguish these deadly flames. The only place to escape from the raging inferno below was to leap off into the unknown.

But what was down there on the forest floor? What the hell would catch him? Would he splat on the ground?

Every time he would be consumed with a fear so ghastly he was left paralysed, unable to move or escape certain death. He knew he should jump. He had to bloody jump! Take a risk... and step off into the unknown. But he could never find the courage to leave the top of his beautiful tree, even though it wasn't safe here anymore.

Every time he would be stuck there, crying and screaming out for someone to save him—but no one ever came. He had no saviours, no heroes here. The smoke would end up getting so thick he could hardly breathe, the fire so hot his skin would bubble and peel and just before the flames would engulf him he would wake up covered in sweat, usually in tears and calling out for help in his empty, lonely house.

Fucking stupid dream.

The only benefit of the hideous nightmare was its habit of striking around the time he would have to get up and start getting ready for work. After calming himself down from his huge scare, Callum would start his day with his morning ritual of planting a kiss on Misty's photograph. Every morning for the past two years he had kissed her face through the glass frame, wishing her luck, praying she would be home soon. Next, he would clamber out of bed and have a shower to wash away the sweat clinging to his body thanks to his night terrors... and then pleasure himself with a wet wank under the hot water.

With the clear mind a brisk morning walk and emptied balls gave him, Callum began to wonder what on earth Garrick had planned for tonight. *What is my punishment for losing?* It was obvious sex was off the menu. Garrick's reluctance on Saturday night to cash in on winning the game of cards made it loud and clear how he had no desire to see Callum's bare ass cleaning again.

As much as this was probably for the best, it didn't stop Callum feeling disappointed to not experience Garrick's magic hands once more. Just one more round of what it felt like to have a hairy, sweaty, muscled body overpower him and ram his hole with a thick cock.

Callum's ass twitched at the thought of how Garrick had impaled him. Owned him. There was something intriguing about the idea of someone else in charge, letting another person call the shots and take control for delivering pleasure. He had always felt a responsibility in the past to please a woman, let her know how beautiful she was... but Garrick had been the one to do that for him. Let Callum know he was beautiful... and loved.

Am I that fucking lonely I could become attracted to my mate? A fresh twinge in his pants gave him the answer. *Yes.* That wasn't the answer he wanted. Nothing good could come from exploring such bizarre feelings. If things were left as they were, he could just put it down to an experience; a one off that didn't mean anything.

It's for the best, Callum told himself. It wasn't like anything more could come from it if he did discover he wasn't entirely straight. He would never date a guy and he certainly wouldn't ever tell anyone about what him and Garrick had done. It wasn't the type of topic you shared with your mates at the tavern or with your family around the dinner table. Sure, it wasn't like he would be chased out of town for admitting such a thing, but it would just be embarrassing. Julie would probably be over the moon to have a gay or bi brother but she would enjoy making fun of him first, he imagined. Then what if his other friends found out?

People like Tim and Johan?

Tim would be in spiteful hysterics to find out Callum had fooled around with a guy. Especially if he knew it was Callum who had been the one receiving. Tim and him may have watched porn together growing up, wanking in the same room, but they had never dared touch each other. And even worse... what if Misty found out? That would be too much.

Nope. Definitely for the best it stays secret.

As Callum rounded the corner onto the main street of town, he noticed a poster glued to a lamp post. It was just a little too dark to make out any real detail but with papers white background and a photo in the middle with writing underneath, he assumed it was some poor local looking for a lost and beloved pet. He continued on up the street spotting the signs every second shop. Finally, he saw the lime green trim of his café's sign hanging from the awning and braced himself for the shift ahead. He fetched the key out of his pocket and went to open the door. Before he could turn the lock, he noticed one of the posters glued to the window of the door.

Holy Fuck!

In a mighty whoosh, all the oxygen escaped Callum's lungs, heart hammering as if he needed Ventolin. "Who the hell..." He looked around the street, trying to see if the person posting signs was around. The street was deserted. He ripped the image off his frontage and quickly screwed it up in his hand. There was no way he was looking at this and there was no way he would be letting anyone else look at this filth either.

He raced up the entire length of the main street, ripping every poster down, gathering them in his pockets to dispose of them privately. He didn't care if he opened up late. He was on big brother duty and Julie needed him to get all of these naked photos of her torn down immediately.

CHAPTER ELEVEN

It took Callum an hour to go around town to find every one of the posters. He was sure he got all of them, but sadly not in time before they were seen by an elderly gentleman walking his dog and two young teenagers ogling the image as they waited for the school bus. The old man was fine and had a chuckle about the image but the school boys had been difficult to wrestle the poster back from, both reluctant to give up a prized possession. In the end Callum had to be aggro with them and shouted, "Hand the fucking poster over now!"

The zitty teens were taken aback by his hostility and both quickly gave up their ruffled pictures of Julie.

"Thank you," Callum had huffed. "If you need porn that fucking badly, I suggest using the internet to have a wank." Both boys' faces turned bright red, too embarrassed to argue.

With all the posters taken down, Callum took them back to the café where Nicky and Jess sat outside waiting to be let in. They asked what was wrong but he dismissed them with a surly look. "Sorry for running late but I've got to go inside and take care of something. Wait out here a minute. I'll come back when it's okay to come in."

Neither questioned him.

Callum raced inside and emptied his pockets of all the screwed-up posters. He wet them in the sink, ripping them into small pieces then turned on the insinkerator to dispose of the shameful evidence.

When he was done, he went back out the front and barked orders at his two staff. "Nicky; I want you to make some fresh cabinet food. Sandwiches, salads, panini's and put out the caramel slice already in the chiller. Jess; you set up the till and if anyone asks for a cooked meal just say that the ovens broken and won't be running 'till after eleven when it's fixed."

"Okay, boss," Nicky replied diligently.

"Is something wrong?" Jess asked, concern warping her pretty face.

"It's nothing, but I have to go out for a while. Run the fort 'till I get back, okay?"

"Okay." Jess nodded.

Callum stepped past them and shook his head as he stomped away angrily. He knew Julie and Graham would be starting work at nine so he would have to hurry. He broke into a sprint and raced the whole way to sister's house. By the time he got to Julie's no-exit street, his side burned with stitch and his mouth cried out for water.

Julie's lockwood home loomed large at the end of the small cul-de-sac. Her and Graham had bought it especially two months ago when they heard Nicky would be coming up to live with them. The place was beautiful and much nicer than Julie's previous rental that her and Graham had shared. This was a real family home with three big bedrooms and a double garage with a self-contained unit attached.

The unit served as Nicky's bedroom, a real gem for any teenager. Callum suspected though, that the unit wasn't so much for Nicky's benefit but for Julie and Graham to have their own space since they still clung to each other like the loved-up couple they were.

Callum walked up the sloping driveway towards the tidy home, climbed the front steps and knocked on the door. His closed fist pounded with pulsating urgency, not caring how rude the rattling clamour of knocks sounded.

"Hold your horses," Julie's voice shrieked out before opening the door. "Callum," She blurted in surprise. She was dressed in a white blouse and black skirt, her blonde hair pulled back in a bun and her face painted in makeup. "What are you doing here? I'm just about to walk out the door so this racket you're making better be important."

Callum stormed in past her, entering the kitchen.

"Yep. It's pretty important," he said in a surly tone.

"Look, if Nicky has done something wrong at the café then speak to Graham about it, I really don't have the time." Julie furrowed her brow, not looking the tiniest bit interested in his impromptu visit.

"It's nothing Nicky has done. It's this!" He reached into his pocket and pulled out a copy of the poster he had saved. He slammed it onto the kitchen counter.

Julie ambled over, looking down with dozy concern 'till she recognised what the poster was of. She snatched it up quickly and gasped. "What the hell is this?"

"You in your birthday suit by the looks and they were plastered all over town."

"They're what? All over town?"

"*Were*," Callum emphasised. "I just spent the past hour ripping them all down."

"Oh my god," Julie whispered, still staring at her nude image. She flashed Callum a quick glance. "Did you get all of them?"

"I think so," Callum grumbled. "Do you have any idea who would have done this?" His blood was stinging. He had a suspect in mind and it pained him to say it out loud. "Is this one of Garrick's pictures?"

"Garrick," Julie squealed. "Why the hell would you think Garrick would have a copy of this?"

"He... he takes pictures of his conquests."

Julie's eyes bulged angrily. "Conquests!"

"People he's sept with."

"Yes, I know what conquests means, Callum," she snapped. "Does it look like Garrick's bedroom to you?"

Callum threw his hands in the air and shook his head. "Sorry, but I didn't exactly spend any time perving at a photo of my sister's amateur attempt at entering the adult entertainment industry."

"Settle down," Julie said. "It's hardly porn and what me and Graham choose to do in our own bedroom is between us."

"Graham?" Callum returned, puzzled.

"Yes, this is a photo taken on my phone. That's our bedroom. Not Garrick's." Julie shook her head in shame. "I lost my phone last week."

"Oh," Callum said. He stared around the kitchen. "Where is Graham?"

"Already left for work," Julie answered before lowering the pitch of her voice to an accusing tone, "Why would you think Garrick would have photos of me?"

"That's what he does. Takes pictures of his... conquests."

Julie laughed. "Does he now... I can assure you that he *never* took such pictures of me."

Callum frowned. "He didn't?"

"No. Never." Julie stared back unperturbed. "And for the record, Callum, Garrick was *my* conquest. Not the other way around. You men all think you're the one doing the banging and never stop to think for even one second that you're getting banged back." She seemed more annoyed about society's sexism than upset about her picture being stapled all over town.

"Shouldn't you be a bit more upset by what I just found plastered all over town?"

"What's worrying about it going to achieve? You said you got them all down, didn't you?"

"Yes, but what if they put them up again?"

"That's their prerogative. If some sad git has nothing better to do than to spread nude pictures of me all over town, then their the one with the problem. Not me."

"How can you be so fucking calm about this." Callum pointed at the poster "It's a nude fucking picture of you for everyone to see."

Julie rolled her eyes. "Callum, I am so grateful to have you as my moody overprotective brother always wanting to look out for me, but trust me this is not one of the times I need you getting your frilly knickers in a twist."

Callum choked on a cough "Excuse me?"

"Yes, I admit it isn't ideal to have these all over town, but it isn't like I have anything to be ashamed about." She shot him a soft smile. "Mum and Dad did right by us by passing on good genes. Why should I be worried about most of the town being jealous about how great I look without my clothes on."

"You're unbelievable," Callum muttered.

"I know right," Julie said, smiling at her photo.

"You know what I mean."

Julie ignored the comment and threw the poster in the rubbish bin by the pantry. She walked over to Callum and gave him a hug. "Thank you for taking them all down. I do appreciate it."

Callum's shoulders knotted in the embrace, he was still annoyed by her carefree response to the shameful pics. "No problem," he grumbled.

Julie let go of him and stepped back. "Look. Come around tonight and I'll make you dinner as a thank you."

"Your cooking's a punishment, not a reward."

Julie whacked his shoulder and giggled. "Sorry we can't all be master chefs like you. If you come 'round I'll make you your favourite meal."

"Do you even know what my favourite meal is?"

Julie shrugged. "Not a clue."

Callum smiled.

"What do you say?" Julie patted his arm.

"I can't tonight, sorry. I am watching the game at Garrick's place."

"Well, how about tomorrow?" Julie tilted her head, trying to be cutesy. "Come on."

"I'll be seeing you tomorrow at Mum and Dad's on Sunday. Won't two nights in a week be a bit of overkill." Callum grinned, letting his sister know he was joking.

"For me maybe. Not for you. You should be grateful every moment you get to spend time in your sister's presence."

"Pfft." Callum laughed. "Okay. I'll come 'round tomorrow night to be poisoned by your culinary skills."

"Brilliant. It'll be nice to have someone else at the dinner table. Between you and me, I hate dinner time with

Graham and Nicky. They constantly talk nonsense that doesn't interest me."

"Like?"

"Cars, sports, current events." Julie screwed her face up. "For once it would be nice to talk about fashion or work place gossip."

"Ha. You think having me there will help bring the table to talk about fashion? Yeah right."

"No, but it will mean you can talk with Nicky so I can have Graham to myself a bit."

"I see. So this reward dinner isn't so much a reward as it I an excuse for you to get a break from playing step mummy."

Julie touched her nose. "Bingo!"

"Nicky seems a nice kid. You should be grateful you're not dealing with some nasty little snot-rag who hates you."

"Who said he doesn't hate me?"

"You think he hates you?"

Julie sighed. "I don't know. I just... I sometimes feel like he ignores me and hijacks Graham's attention too much."

"You mean you're not used to not being the centre of attention." Callum loved his sister but he knew she was guilty of being self-centred.

"It's not just that. He just tends to always be around. If he isn't at work then he is here, moping about the house."

"Umm, how is that a problem?"

"He's seventeen, Callum. What teenager wants to hang around his father *all* the time. It isn't normal."

"He's new to town, Julie, he probably needs a bit more time to get out and make some mates. Besides, you were the one who wanted to date a guy twice your age who already had a kid. I think this just comes with the territory." Callum and his parents did warn Julie about the age gap and the responsibility that came with dating Graham, but like every other bit of advice given Julie's way, she chose to ignore it.

"Graham is not twice my age he's 45," Julie said in a

defensive tone. She slumped her shoulders and muttered, "You're right. I'm probably just being selfish."

Callum nodded, smiling at his sister. "Probably. Look on the Brightside though. One more year and you will have Graham all to yourself again."

"You think?"

"Yeah. Nicky should have made some mates by then and moved into a flat of his own. Then you'll have your old crusty boyfriend all to yourself again."

Julie whacked his shoulder again. "Graham is not old and crusty."

"If you say so. Just don't come complaining to be when you start coughing up grey fur balls." Callum stepped back so his sister couldn't attack him with another playful hit.

"Gross!" Julie shrieked with laughter. "Right. You and me both have to get going to work before I strangle you."

"An amateur porn star and a wannabe murderer. Mum and Dad must be so proud." Callum grinned at his sister.

"Yes, well we can't all be the golden child like you."

Callum pretended to brush dust off his shoulders. "What can I say? Being everyone's favourite just comes naturally to me."

"Yeah, right," Julie scoffed. "Aside from Mum and Dad and maybe your bum buddy Garrick, I think your list of being number one ends there."

Callum's stomach tightened. "Don't be fucking disgusting," he snapped.

Julie frowned, surprised by his hostile response. "Calm down, I was only joking about your boy's bromance."

"Sorry," Callum apologised, knowing he had overreacted. He coughed up a guilty smile. "I'll see you tomorrow night, yeah?"

"Yes, you will," Julie said.

Callum hugged his sister goodbye and left to head back to work, trying to ignore the imaginary throbbing in his ass brought on by Julie innocently saying what Garrick actually was… Callum's *bum buddy*.

CHAPTER TWELVE

Callum found himself with butterflies of excitement in his chest. If they fluttered any harder then there was every chance his feet might just leave the ground. He was on his way to Garrick's place to watch the rugby match and it felt like he was walking on fluffy clouds of dreams. After the ordeal with Julie's naked spread all over town, he had managed to calm himself down by returning to work and focusing on the highlight of his Tuesday night. *Garrick.*

He was always excited to go hang out with his mate but since their experimental descent into lovemaking, Callum found the impending visit more thrilling. Saturday night's disappointment of no sex had been a dampener to his emerging curiosity but he tried to focus on the bright side. Even if they never had sex again, Callum had found some sort of treasure in what they had done; a rare gem of love he didn't know existed between them. Garrick would go on shagging every female he could, but that would never take away from the memory they had created together.

When he got to Garrick's apartment, Callum could see his mate upstairs on the balcony; his silhouette illuminated by the last shreds of daylight dangling in the sky.

Garrick leant over the side, giving a mock salute. "Come on up, buddy. Door's unlocked."

Callum smiled and walked on in, making his way upstairs to join his mate. When he stepped onto the deck, he found Garrick bent over a long terracotta tray, planting what looked to be vegetable seedlings. He wore a rumpled, white shirt with the sleeves rolled up and the tails untucked over a pair of black gym shorts. Even in such sloppy attire he could still leave the house and turn heads.

"Hey, man." Callum smiled at his pal and took a seat

on a green plastic seat. "Whatcha doing?"

Garrick stood up straight, swivelling 'round. "Just plating some lettuce and broccoli plants."

"I didn't pick you as the green-fingered type."

"I'm not usually." He flashed a quick smile. "Unless it's a particularly nasty yeast infection."

Callum's eyes crinkled with laughter. "Fucking gross."

Garrick smiled, wiping his brow. "Nar. I just figured it would be cool to try and grow my own veges this season."

"I wish I had a garden to do that."

"You do, Callum. You have an entire fucking empty back yard." Garrick laughed. "If I can do this on just my balcony then you could easily do the same."

"True."

"Why haven't you tried having a garden?" Garrick asked.

"Misty never wanted a garden."

"How come?" Garrick frowned.

Callum coughed up an embarrassed laugh. "She said she wanted us to have plenty of space for stuff like a trampoline and swing set for when we had kids."

Garrick gave a commiserating look. "Well, the bitch is gone now. If you want a garden then have a bloody garden."

"She wasn't a bitch," Callum said defensively.

Garrick's lip quirked. "According to your sister she was a nightmare."

"Julie would say that," Callum scoffed.

"Hmm." He wiped his dirt-caked hands down his shorts. "Why's that?"

"They never got along. The whole time me and Misty were together Julie was bitter about it."

Bitter was probably an understatement. Both women hated one another from high school days when they had fought over the same boy.

Garrick nodded. "I'm guessing Julie was over the moon when you split up then?"

"You could say that." Callum smiled, remembering Julies juvenile revenge after Misty had broken his heart. In the middle of the night she had gone and spray painted badly-drawn spunking cocks all over Misty's parents' driveway. He had hit the roof when he heard what she had done, but he knew this was Julie's way of trying to defend his honour... even if it was misguided.

"Maybe it's time you start this garden, buddy."

Callum nodded, not wanting to agree out loud with something Misty would not approve of.

Garrick gestured towards a box of RTD vodka bottles on the table beside Callum. "Help yourself to a drink."

"Are you sure?" Callum hadn't planned on drinking. He didn't want to keep bleeding his pal dry.

"I wouldn't offer if I didn't mean it," Garrick said sternly, sounding like a teacher. He followed up in a softer voice, "What's mine is yours."

Callum dipped a hand in the box, retrieving a bottle. "How long until kick off?"

"We have another half hour yet. Should be a good match," Garrick said, staring out at the harbour.

Callum didn't respond, casting his eyes to his friend's ridiculously handsome face. He focused on Garrick's lips—such pretty and heavenly lips which had done devilish things to him just the other night. He quickly flicked his eyes away when Garrick turned around.

"So how was your day?" Garrick asked.

"Another day, another dollar. You know the story." Callum didn't want to go into the whole Julie poster scandal. He had felt guilty for thinking Garrick would be responsible. It was ludicrous to think Garrick would do something like that. However, it still bothered Callum not knowing who would have pulled that kind of stunt.

Garrick scratched at his knee, shivering slightly from the evening breeze licking his skin. "Shall we head inside and set up for the game?"

"Sounds good to me."

Garrick went and picked the box of drinks up and headed inside.

Callum, clutching his drink of vodka, followed behind

him, letting his eyes burn on Garrick's firm rear. When they had been naked together, Callum had been so wrapped up with the orgasmic pleasure being given to him that he hadn't had the chance to check out Garrick's ass. A horny disappointment gnawed at him now for missing the opportunity. He wished he had been given a turn to do the fucking; a chance to show Garrick his own manoeuvres.

I'd fuck you so good, mate. So fucking good…

In the lounge the large television screen was already blaring with pre-commentary about the looming match. On the coffee table Callum spotted Garrick's laptop. The screen saver was on and displaying one of Garrick's conquests. The star of the show was a pretty Maori woman with large breasts and caramel coloured skin. She had a blanket draped over her lower half to provide at least some modesty. Knowing that the random female was not his sister, Callum let his eyes admire the naked body and the background of the shot.

Definitely Garrick's bedroom.

Up until this morning Callum had always enjoyed seeing Garrick's screensaver pics, letting his eyes ogle whatever beauty was on the screen. Now though he had a twinge of guilt as he wondered if this was someone else's sister. He knew how enraged a brother would be to discover that their sibling was plastered on some dude's computer. A supposedly innocent picture between lovers that at the time the woman would have had no clue about how Garrick would be adding it to his *collection.*

They sat down together on the couch, prime spectating position for the televised match.

"Is she your latest addition, is she?" Callum raised his eyebrows, pointing to the laptop screen.

"Not recent but one of my favs," Garrick said, placing the box of drinks on the floor by his feet.

She would have to be one of his favs to be the screensaver shot. Callum knew that Garrick had tonnes of women hidden away in secret folders on his computer. Only the cream of the crop got a starring role as the screensaver.

"I can see why," Callum said, taking a seat on the

couch next to his mate.

"Yeah. That was Ariana. Fucking demon in the sack." Garrick licked his lips like he could still taste her. "Love a girl who isn't afraid to let loose, if you know what I mean?"

Callum gulped. "Yeah. I know what you mean."

He didn't really know what Garrick meant. His experience with women was tame and sensual. He found himself look over quickly at Garrick's crotch. His stomach turned when he realised that both he and this Ariana had let Garrick inside of them. *Even my sister has had him inside her.* The thought was a heavy one.

"How many people have you slept with?" Callum blurted. Knowing he was on Garrick's list made him want to know how many others had come before him.

Garrick shrugged. "I dunno. I never really kept track."

"How does the guy who keeps a collection not know how many people he's shagged?"

"I only started the collection after uni so it doesn't include everyone."

Callum thought of what Julie had said. How she had never let Garrick take her picture. "Is Julie on there?"

Garrick laughed. "No mate. Even if she was, I wouldn't have her as my screensaver out of respect to you."

"So how come you don't have her photo?" He felt stupid for asking but he was curious to know more about his friend's mating rituals.

Garrick took a deep breath. "I only take pictures of the girls I've fucked in my bed. You probably don't wanna know this but me and ya sister never made it to the bedroom before we ripped one another's clothes off."

"Oh god," Callum muttered.

Garrick laughed. "I told you, you wouldn't want to know."

"So how many people do you *think* you have slept with? Just a ball park figure?"

"You seem rather interested all of a sudden." Garrick narrowed his eyes to thin slits. "Is it because…"

Callum blushed. He was grateful Garrick didn't finish

the sentence. It was the closest they had been to talking about what they had done. "I'm just curious."

"I would say it's triple digits."

"Triple-fucking-digits!" Callum's mouth gaped open. "Holy fuck."

Garrick smirked, amused by the shock on Callum's face. "I can't help being popular."

"There's popular and then there's... *that*," Callum said.

"Settle down, Mother Theresa. I'm just a young guy who likes to have fun. Ain't nothing wrong with having fun."

"Don't you worry about diseases?"

"Aside from pissing razor blades once a few years back, I can't say I've had any issues."

Callum groaned internally. "Charming."

Garrick shook his head, smiling. "If you're worried about it because of what we did together then I can assure you not to worry. I always play safe and I get my sexual warrant of fitness checked regularly."

"I would hope so," Callum replied, sounding like a parent. He looked over and gave Garrick an apologetic look. "Sorry. I don't mean to sound like a dick."

"It's okay. I know the concern comes from a place of caring... and being jealous."

"Ha. Jealous. Jealous of what?"

"Of getting laid as much as me."

"Yeah right," Callum scoffed.

Truth was he did feel a tinge of jealousy. He may have been two years older but he was the junior in the sex department.

Garrick rubbed his shoulder. "It's okay, mate. Not everyone can be a stud."

Callum laughed, nudging Garrick with his elbow. "Whatever. I'm all about quality, not quantity."

"Yep. And you took every inch of the best quality there is."

Whatever invisible line there had been lingering between them, forcing them not to specifically mention the deed had just been obliterated. Callum looked down at his feet. Too nervous to look his ass fucker in the face.

"My cock is high quality, don't you think?" Garrick's voice dropped to sexy levels.

Callum relented, looking him in the eyes.

Garrick's lips curled into a sneer and he groped himself blatantly.

"I'm straight, Garrick, so I don't know if I can comment."

"But can you really still say that after the other night?"

"Yes," Callum replied instinctively. "What we did was just some drunken silly shit. I'm not saying I didn't have fun—because I did, we both did—but that doesn't mean I'm no longer straight."

Garrick's eyes pinged with cheek and he nodded slowly, almost mockingly. "If you say so."

"What's that supposed to mean?"

"If I told you that your punishment for losing cards on Saturday was to suck my cock then you would tell me to fuck off, would you?" He took a well-timed sip on his bottle of booze. "You know, 'cos you're so straight and all."

Fuuuuuuuck! Callum felt his chest tighten. He searched his mind for the right way to answer. A part of him wanted nothing more than to fool around again, but his staunch male pride refused to dignify the accusation. He was on a sexual tightrope and he didn't want to fall off either side.

"Between you and me, Callum, I think you rather enjoyed having my dick rammed in your tight ass." Garrick tugged on the waistband of his shorts, looking down at his popular prick. "He is a handsome fucker so no one could blame you." He let go and his shorts made a sharp snapping sound as the waistband slapped back against his skin.

"Fancy lowering the ego a bit," Callum said. "I know who I am, Garrick, and who I am isn't gay." The words came out all too pleading and it was clear Garrick could sense this.

"Not even a tincy wincy bit?"

Callum let out a hot breath, not answering. He took a sip of his drink.

"Just so you know, that is your punishment by the way," Garrick said. "Sucking my cock."

Callum glared at him. "You want me to suck your dick?"

"Yes. And you can say thank you for the privilege since I know it ain't much of a punishment for you."

"Piss off. I ain't saying thank you for *that*." Callum laughed. "And, newsflash; I'm not sucking your dick." He had no choice but to play up how supposedly unwilling he was. He couldn't risk Garrick knowing how strong his curiosity to explore had become. Yes, he had enjoyed it, and yes, he had wanted to do more, but he wasn't letting his cocky pal try and put him in a box and label him something he wasn't.

"You will say thank you because I am only letting you suck it if you do."

Callum rolled his eyes. "You're crazy, man."

"Am I?" Garrick leant forward, resting his elbows on his knees. "So I'm crazy thinking that you lost the game of cards on purpose?"

CHAPTER THIRTEEN

Callum's body jolted like he had been zapped. "What?"

"You didn't lose that game. You won," Garrick said flatly. "When you went for a piss, I checked your cards and I saw the hand you had. You beat me."

Callum sucked his bottom lip. He had been busted. Busted badly. His insides squirmed as he waited for where this was going.

"Now why would you lose that game on purpose? I know you like winning as much as the next guy." Garrick tapped him on the arm. "Come on, why'd you let me win?"

"I just felt like you deserved to win. I was being a mate."

Garrick threw his head back and laughed. "Don't speak such crap. I know you better than that. You'd never lose a game to try and make me feel better."

"Maybe you don't know me as well as you think," Callum hissed, raising the bottle to his lips again.

"Oh, I think I do. I know you *intimately* Callum Bradshaw." Garrick smiled. "Look, I don't care what you are, all I want is my dick sucked." He tugged at the crotch of his shorts so hard Callum could see the plump ridge of his dick through the material.

"Fuck, don't overdose on the romance."

"This isn't about romance," Garrick said. "This is about two guys sitting alone and one of them just happens to want his dick sucked."

Callum shook his head, losing his patience with Garrick's mind games. "Okay, I admit it. I lost the game on purpose to see if we would try stuff again. I had fun and I wanted to see if I'd have fun again if we had a repeat.

Happy?"

Garrick nodded. "I'm so hot I made you wanna try stuff again. Of course that makes me happy."

"Do you want a fucking medal or something?"

"No. You sucking my cock is the only medal I need."

"For Christ's sake, Garrick, do you have to be so crass about it?"

"Sorry, I'm just kidding." He gave Callum a warm smile. "So you really enjoyed me fucking you? For real?"

Callum scratched his ear, delaying his response. "I enjoyed sharing something special with you."

"Aww, that's a little bit sweet."

"Don't make fun of me, please," Callum huffed, exasperation creeping into his voice.

"But I do think it's sweet. I mean, it is kind of gay but still pretty sweet."

"Two things; firstly, I didn't fuck myself, you were there too so that makes you just as gay as me. And secondly, I am not actually claiming to be gay, I am just saying it was an experience that I enjoyed."

Garrick chuckled, getting a kick out of how rattled Callum was sounding. "I hear ya. But how much do you want to do it again?"

"What do you mean?" Callum asked, playing coy.

"How badly do you want to suck my cock for me?" Garrick flicked his eyes down at his bulge. "You can suck me off right now if you want, but you have to say thank you."

Garrick's power trip was infuriating.

Callum cast him a stormy glare but Garrick wasn't budging; his eyes demanded that Callum obey. Against his inner pride's wishes, Callum capitulated. "Fine. *Thank you, Garrick,* for letting me suck your cock again," he muttered sarcastically.

"That wasn't so hard now, was it?" Contempt oozed from his voice.

"No," Callum grumbled.

"Good man." Garrick pointed to the centre of the room. "Now stand over there and get naked."

"Are you serious?"

"Go over there and take all your clothes off," Garrick repeated.

Callum put his drink down and heaved himself off of the couch. As resentful as he was feeling, some intense desire forced him to do as he was told. He stood in the desired spot and took his shoes and socks off. Hesitating, he glimpsed over and saw Garrick smirking.

"Keep going. I want you naked."

Callum let out a defeated breath. He cocked his head to the left and then the right, like a bird looking out for a predator. He stripped away the rest of his clothes 'till he was standing buck ass naked in the centre of the room, glaring angrily. He covered his crotch with his hands, attempting to reinforce the lie portrayed on his face.

"Take your hands away. I wanna see your dick," Garrick said firmly.

Callum peeled his hands away, revealing his true feelings about the unfolding scene.

"Fucking hell, you already got yaself a stiffy going on." Garrick laughed and patted his crotch. "I better not deny you what you want. Come on over."

In small, ponderous steps, Callum migrated towards his master, hunkering down in front of his open legs. He stared at the mound in his shorts. He looked up and asked, "Don't you need to get naked?"

"Nar, mate. I only need to take my shorts off. I plan on watching the game while you suck me."

"The whole game?"

"Yep. I've always wanted to be sucked off while I kick back watching the rugby with a cold one in my hand."

"But I wanted to watch the game too."

"Tough luck. You have a job to do." Garrick's sordid command was as sexy as it was derogatory.

Callum felt his cock twitch. He stared at Garrick's strong thighs. He was gagging to feel the manly limbs under his hands while he sucked him off. He had already been outed for wanting to do this. It seemed pointless to try and debate the fact now that he was naked and sat between his mate's legs. He gave a slight nod of the head, accepting his role as cock sucker for the evening.

Garrick lifted his butt off the couch and pulled his shorts and briefs right down to his ankles, flicking them away with his left foot. His dick was flaccid and lay atop of his fuzzy balls. The darkness of his wiry pubes was in stark contrast to the paleness of his meat. He sat so confidently, so at ease, like having his dick out was no big deal.

Callum craned his neck forward and dipped his face down. He started slowly, cautiously, tracing his tongue from Garrick's knee up his inner thigh. He nuzzled into the crease of Garrick's groin, breathing in. His crotch was ripe with a thick, musty smell. Callum pushed apart Garrick's thighs, needy and hungry for more of his pal's signature aroma. He chased the scent along Garrick's balls, licking and tasting, absorbing him.

He run his palms up and down Garrick's shins, warming the skin. When he had finally had his fill of ball sweat, he scooped Garrick's soft meat inside his mouth and sucked.

Garrick pat him on the head like he was a pet. He drew his knees in, pressing them against Callum's shoulders, locking him in.

Callum sucked and sucked, getting a thrill from the way Garrick's dick responded so quickly to his wet mouth. Every twitch and jerk of his mate's growing girth made Callum's own cock throb. It didn't take long for Callum to become fully erect and it wasn't much longer before Garrick's cock joined his own in the rock-hard department.

Callum slurped and slobbered over the thick manhood, desperate to ram as much of Garrick in his mouth as possible. In the background he could hear the whistle for kick off sounding.

Garrick leant forward, grabbing a drink from the box, his stomach pressing down on the top of Callum's head, forcing more dick in Callum's mouth and making him gag and choke. Garrick chuckled, leaning back. "Bit of a mouthful, is it?"

Callum pulled his mouth off. "You could say that." He looked up to see Garrick grinning.

"You probably wish your cock was as big as mine," Garrick said cruelly.

"Yes," Callum admitted, holding Garrick's blessed proportion in his hand.

"I thought as much," He clicked his fingers. "Get back to sucking."

Callum plopped his mouth back over his mate's cock, sucking like he was told to. The whole situation was fucked-up. This wasn't like the other night when they were both drunk, exploring new waters as equals. Tonight was all on Garrick's terms and the dark-haired stud was making it known he was the one in charge with a dismissive attitude which felt purposely designed to make Callum feel inferior. It was working. Callum was feeling inferior. However, something in him was finding this a turn on, knowing he had a job to do, knowing his place.

Callum's mouth was pooling up with spit the more he tried taking Garrick in. He slurped back loudly, sucking back up his dribbling spit. The sexy noise had an effect on Garrick; his dick throbbed, swelling even more inside Callum's mouth. His hands continued to roam up and down Garrick's toned legs, absorbing the hairy and muscular terrain. It was potently male what he was experiencing. No smooth skin or supple breasts in sight, just a hard, thick rod and manly features beneath his frisky fingers.

I really fucking enjoy this, Callum told himself. He had his answer. The odd feelings he had been having for Garrick since last week weren't imagined—the physical attraction was real. As his jaw ached from sucking endlessly through the match playing on television, Callum wasn't sure if he was relieved or scared to know that he found male traits attractive. A brief moment of dizziness came over him, it was scary to discover something so personal about himself.

Why didn't I fucking know about this already?

It seemed strange to be 28 years-old and only just now

discover he was turned on by men. Well, by Garrick at least. At no point during their friendship had he thought of Garrick in this way, never contemplated that one day he would be naked between this man's legs, sucking his cock, whiffing his ball sweat.

Callum was sucking best he could, his tongue swirling along the meaty underside of Garrick's shaft, sucking wetly on his magnificent manhood. He was desperate to hear Garrick say how amazing he was and that he was about to cum. Such praise and warnings weren't coming though.

Garrick sat back quite normally, shouting at the referee and the players, egging them on to get their shit together and score a try. Aside from the occasional moan he behaved like Callum wasn't even there between his legs. After twenty minutes, Callum's mouth grew tired and he wondered if he should give up, spit Garrick's dick out and say he was done.

But then like he could sense the dying enthusiasm, Garrick's hand stroked the side of Callum's face. "You're doing a good job, buddy. Keep it up," he whispered and then twirled his fingers through Callum's hair. "Lick my balls a bit. I love it when my balls are licked."

The praise and hair twirling was like a shot of energy being injected into Callum's veins. He lapped it up and promptly moved his mouth down to Garrick's fuzzy balls and tongued at his mate's sac; his efforts earning a sigh of pleasure from Garrick's lips. He felt Garrick's thick rod dab his forehead as he dug his tongue under Garrick's musky balls.

"Fuck yeah, Callum. That's the shit."

Callum dragged his tongue low, digging deep under Garrick's balls, lashing the tip of his taint. Garrick's legs jiggled around, reacting to the sensual prostate prodding.

"Stop," Garrick moaned but Callum ignored him, too horny to obey. Garrick ripped him by the hair gruffly. "I said, fucking stop!" He pulled Callum's face back and stared back with eyes so sharp and angry they could cut glass. "I don't want to cum just yet. Go back to sucking my dick."

Callum nodded and plopped his mouth back over Garrick's cock like he was fucking it. He rode the wave of energy, going on and on, until he heard Garrick clap his hands.

"It's half time, mate. Time for a smoke break," Garrick said, pulling Callum off his cock. He smiled warmly. "You're getting good at this."

"Ha. Thanks." Callum chuckled. "After that long I probably should be though."

"Not everyone can suck a dick as good as that. I reckon you were born to be a cock sucker."

Callum cringed. The compliment nipped with a sour sting.

"You stay here," Garrick said. "I'm gonna go outside have a smoke and when I come back I'll let you finish me off." He stood up, stepping around Callum and wandered off towards outside with his bare ass on show.

Callum quickly swivelled his head 'round to admire Garrick's ass. His buttocks were firm and milky white, his crack a shadowy line scattered with dark hair. He sat in a daze, waiting for Garrick to return. He looked down between his legs and saw how rock hard he was, the tip of his penis drooling precum. If he didn't have to sort Garrick out then he would have tugged himself off, emptying his balls of the humungous pleasure welling within him.

"Right, that's my lungs taken care of," Garrick said loudly as he reappeared in the lounge. "I was thinking you can finish me off in the bedroom." He flicked his eyes towards the hallway door.

"Wh-what about the game?" Callum sputtered.

"It's been a bit one-sided so far, so it ain't exactly a surprise who will win."

"Oh." Callum had no idea the match was going that way, he had been too busy with his face buried sucking dick. The invite to the bedroom felt personal, a bed would make this all so much more intimate, he thought. *We might make love like last time.* Callum got to his feet and got a shock when Garrick reached out with no warning, gripping hold of his cock.

"Let's get you back to work," Garrick said, his hot breath wafting over Callum's face. He squeezed Callum's erection, licking his lips.

Callum looked his mate in the eyes and stupidly asked, "Would I be allowed to fuck you this time?"

Garrick squeezed him tighter and laughed with disdain. "If there's any fucking going on then it's me fucking you. That's the way this goes."

Is it? Callum's heart sank a little. "What is this exactly?"

"*This* is me doing you a favour. You're the one whose gagging for it. Not me.

Callum was gobsmacked. He was embarrassed by the truth of the statement; a blush rose on his cheeks and he looked towards the wall to avoid meeting Garrick's eyes.

"So since I am being such a nice guy and willing to help you out," Garrick tapped him on the shoulder, "I'll be the one doing the fucking."

Callum reluctantly returned his gaze.

Garrick stared back at him with a shit-eating grin on his face, his entire body smouldering with sex appeal. "We can stop now if you want. It's no skin off my nose. I can just as easily go to bed after you leave and have a wank. But if you want this, then I suggest you march your ass down to my bedroom and get on all fours so I can fuck you properly."

Callum clenched his jaw, wanting to yell back. The way Garrick spoke made Callum feel like some sort of pity fuck.

Then it dawned on him. *This is a pity fuck!*

Garrick was the one with all the power in this exchange. If Callum wanted to experience Garrick's passion again then he had to give up his own expectations of what that passion would be. Everything about the cocky bastard kept opening Callum's eyes to new desires. He couldn't fight it. Callum swallowed his pride and nodded his head, lowering himself to a level he didn't think he would ever be capable of. *Yes*—he would take the pity fuck.

Garrick leant in and pecked Callum on the lips. "Now get that hot ass of yours to my room while I look for my phone."

"Your phone?"

"I'm about to fuck you in my bed, buddy, that means you get added to the collection."

Whoa! Suddenly shit felt all too real. All too serious. He had spent the morning ripping down the damage that could be done with private photos. He started to shake his head. "I-I don't know if I can do—"

Garrick grabbed him by the shoulders and silenced him with a kiss. He pulled away and said, "The pictures are for my eyes only, Callum. No one else will ever see them. I promise. I have a reputation to upkeep myself." He waggled his eyebrows. "Do you think I'd be able to take pictures of everyone I slept with if I didn't know how to be discrete?"

Garrick raised a good point. He wouldn't have been able to get away with such kinks had he not learnt the importance of keeping secrets. However, Callum knew that he'd have to be pretty dumb and desperate to actually agree to this–to give Garrick such bragging rights.

He nibbled on his lip, taking his time to think it over.

Finally, he stepped around Garrick and marched to the hallway. Callum decided he wasn't smart. He was dumb. Dumb and horny. He walked swiftly towards Garrick's bedroom, leading the way, ready to become the newest addition in his best mate's dubious collection.

CHAPTER FOURTEEN

Callum entered Garrick's darkened bedroom and reached for the light switch, flicking it on and drowning the room with a stream of brightness. Normally, Callum had never paid much attention to his mate's bedroom before. It was just a room, nothing important about it. But knowing it would be the scene of the second time he would take Garrick's cock inside him, everything about the room was important and up for scrutiny.

Callum's eyes flitted around in all directions, taking in every detail of the large room. The pale white walls were decorated with strategically placed pictures—mostly landscape photos—and a burst of colour that came in the form of a psychedelic paisley wall hanging. The room smelled clean and fresh despite the mess of strewn clothes.

Callum scanned the floor, noticing the used rubber was gone. He spotted a pair of green briefs sitting atop a pair of worn jeans snaked out on the floor. He had a strange thrill blitz his senses when he made the odd connection that he had just been sucking the very body parts the briefs had been wrapped around.

Next, his eyes wandered to the mattress, leaving him hypnotised, like it was about to be a space of self-sacrifice. The white pillows looked soft and innocent compared to the tussled black sheets. It was only when Garrick walked into the room, holding his phone, that Callum became unglued from his mesmerised state.

"What are ya waiting for?" Garrick said, fiddling with the phone in his hands. "On the bed. All fours." His tone was crisp and utterly dismissive.

Callum looked over his shoulder at Garrick holding the phone like a loaded gun. Only now did he fully appreciate how different him and Garrick's sexual tastes were. Callum was turned on by intimacy, Garrick by control. He wasn't quite sure how well these two things would mesh. Still, he gave in, giving his mate what he wanted.

Callum clambered onto the mattress, assuming the position—head down, ass pointing out. His chest heaved with an anxious breath, a fusion of lustful wanting and fear for what was to come. He took a series of deep breaths as he stared down at the twisted black sheets beneath him. He could hear Garrick stepping closer to the end of the bed. Callum flinched when Garrick's hand touched his rump.

"Someone's a bit jumpy," Garrick said with a soft chuckle. His hand slid over the smooth mounds of Callum's ass cheeks, settling a finger at the tip of his crack that he then dragged down the middle like he was inspecting the hidden depth. "Are you looking forward to me putting my cock inside here," Garrick said, prodding Callum's tight hole with his finger.

Callum nodded.

"Good." Garrick finished his statement by slapping Callum's butt.

The sting of the slap made Callum wince. Garrick's hands were capable of giving just as much pain as they were pleasure. This felt like a risk. But it would be worth it. Callum needed this like he had never needed anything before in his whole life.

"I want you to spread your cheeks apart for me," Garrick said.

Callum craned his neck 'round, glaring back at Garrick who stood confidently with just his shirt on, his erection jutting forward like an arrow.

"Spread your cheeks," Garrick repeated. "I wanna take some pics of this hot ass I'm about to fuck."

Callum gulped from the sound of his mate's words which were as blunt as his tone. He lowered his face onto the mattress and reached around and clutched his cheeks, opening himself up. His breath sped up to match the galloping rhythm of his heart. He waited for Garrick to say something, compliment him maybe? But no, there was nothing said.

Click. Click. Click. Click. Click. Click.

Callum lost count the amount of times he heard the phone click, capturing images of his ass and hairy crack splayed open.

Garrick appeared at the side of the bed and begun taking shots from a new angle. Callum buried his face so it was hidden, he had no intention of letting Garrick put his face in the pictures.

"Play with your cock a bit. I wanna see it in your hand," Garrick said.

With his face still mostly-buried for privacy, Callum grabbed between his legs, tugging on his cock as instructed. Garrick lowered himself and positioned the camera closer to get a snap of the dick-pulling action. Suddenly, Callum noticed that the camera wasn't making a clicking noise anymore.

The fucker is actually recording a video!

Callum's stomach twirled. Videos weren't supposed to be on the menu. He wanted to say something but he didn't want his voice being captured and archived as part of the ordeal. His silence made no difference it turned out.

"Mmm, this sexy fucker on my bed playing with his cock is Callum—"

"Why the hell are you talking," Callum snapped, his voice muffled in the sheets.

Garrick chuckled. "I like to have a bit of running commentary."

"Aren't photos and video enough?"

"Relax, mate. I told you, it's only me who ever sees this."

Callum sighed loudly, venting his frustration but agreeing to the path Garrick was dictating. His pride slipping away like a landslide.

Garrick patted Callum's shoulder and continued with his raunchy ramblings, "Normally I don't do dudes but Callum's my *best mate* and he seems a bit fixated on my cock and has asked me to fuck him tonight, and being the good guy I am, I thought I'd oblige and give my buddy here what he wants so badly."

Callum swore his face was glowing like hot coals from the story Garrick was spinning. The worst part was, none of it was a lie.

"Yep. He just sucked me off for nearly an hour in the lounge. He sucks dick like a pro, may I add."

Callum felt a slight zing of pride ripple within him from the dodgy praise being bestowed upon him.

"You're really keen to be fucked, aren't ya?" Garrick stared at Callum, waiting for him to respond.

Callum offered back a limp nod.

"Speak up. I can't hear a nod." Garrick said.

"I'm really keen to be fucked by you, Garrick." The words hurt as much to say as the slap he'd received to the ass.

"Come here," Garrick said. "Show me how good you are at sucking my cock."

Callum's lips pressed together, trapping a bottled-up moan, his body stiffened, hesitant to move.

"Come on, man. Don't be shy," Garrick whispered. He stroked the nape of Callum's neck.

The sensual stroke was enough to make Callum crumble, he raised his face and shuffled his body around to face Garrick standing at the edge of the bed. He kept his eyes on his mate's cock, not daring to peep at the phone in Garrick's hands. He held Garrick's firm thighs and guided his face down and opened his mouth, slipping orally over the slight curve of Garrick's cock.

"Fuck yeah," Garrick muttered, slowly fucking Callum's mouth with a gentle sway of his hips. He gripped a tuft of Callum's blond hair, pulling tight, making sure his mouth remained locked in place and available. Each light shove Garrick fed, gave Callum an extra inch that made him gag and dribble with spit.

Callum clawed at Garrick's legs, digging his blunt nails into the skin, indulging in his cock-sucking role.

"Look at me," Garrick grumbled. "I want you to look

me in the eyes while you suck me."

Callum tilted his face up and saw Garrick's lush lips curled at the edges with a sexy smirk. Their eyes meeting was intense. Yes, he was enjoying this but having to look his mate in the eyes was unnerving—it hammered home just how submissive he was being... and with whom.

Garrick's midnight-eyes roared with confidence, a glint of conceit dancing in his dark pupils. "Say cheese," he said, lifting the camera.

Click.

Callum's face gobbing on a dick was caught on film. Now Garrick had the most scandalous photo imaginable. He kept clicking in delight, taking shot after shot of Callum's wide-eyed submission and cock-filled lips. Superstitious beliefs that a photo could take a piece of a person's soul didn't feel so farfetched anymore. Each click made Callum feel like Garrick was chipping away another piece of him.

"Time to give you what you really want," Garrick said. He pushed Callum's face back, retrieving his spit-soaked dick. "Spin 'round. I'm gonna fuck you now."

Again, Callum was caught off guard by just how demeaning Garrick was being to him. The tenderness from the other night he was craving so badly was just not there. *I really should get up and leave.* But his cock was raging even harder than before. Something about this derogatory exchange was affecting him. And it wasn't entirely negative. In clumsy fashion, he rotated his body around, his ass now facing Garrick, ready for his fucking.

Garrick's hand touched his ass softly, tickling him with his fingertips before launching another surprise attack with a hefty slap.

"Argh fuck!" Callum cried out.

"Sorry, buddy. I just couldn't resist." Garrick's moist breath blew over Callum's stinging skin, followed by a tiny kiss.

The small gesture provided a big remedy. If Garrick promised to kiss him after each slap then Callum would have let his mate wail on him. He could feel the heat from

Garrick's body humming behind him, Callum prayed that his mate would lean forward and lay atop of him, skin to skin.

Cover my body with all of you.

Callum heard Garrick moving away from the bed, he turned his face to see Garrick placing the phone down on the small bedside table then begin to rummage in one of the drawers. Garrick reached in, grabbing out a blue condom packet and a small bottle of lubricant. Callum quickly flicked his face back to focusing on the mattress, not wanting Garrick to catch him peeping. With his eyes remained fixed on the bedsheets, Callum only had the sense of sound to gauge how close Garrick's cock was to entering him.

The first signal was the ripping open of the condom packet. The next clue was the peeling off of Garrick's shirt which he dropped on the bed next to Callum. Finally, the sound of squirting lube filled the air and Callum shivered as the cold, sticky residue was wiped down his crack and lathered into his hole.

"Fuck, I hate getting this shit on my hands," Garrick complained. He wiped his slimy hand down Callum's flank, using him like a towel. "Good thing I can use you as a rag."

Callum didn't complain. It felt part of the deal.

Garrick grabbed hold of Callum's hips, steering his cock to the start of its journey.

As soon as the tip of his mate's cock nudged his quivering hole, Callum jolted and his sphincter clenched.

"Relax, mate," Garrick said, halting the inevitable penetration. "You know I start easy."

"I know," Callum whispered, dry-mouthed now. He wondered how his ass looked right now with a thick, hard cock hovering between his cheeks.

"On the count of three... one... two..." Garrick didn't wait for three and pushed forward, sliding his cock inside with careless pressure.

Callum sucked in a gust of wind and began panting from the painful intrusion.

You said you'd go fucking easy!

Garrick started rubbing his lower back almost like an

apology. Tender touches designed to silence any aggrieved feelings.

Callum kept breathing in and out, trying to adjust to having at least two inches of fuckmeat sheathed inside him. Garrick gave another firm shove, gaining more territory. Callum's eyes watered and he mashed his lips together. Then, out of nowhere, Garrick rammed forward, forcing his cock all the way in, skewering Callum's tight ass.

"Ough," Callum hissed, about to spew a string of curse words, but Garrick reached around and smothered his hand over Callum's lips, shutting his mouth.

Garrick pushed him forward on the bed then lay all his weight atop of him, draping his body over Callum's back, forcing him to lay down flat.

Callum twitched and shivered, a sexy grogginess overpowering him from being trapped beneath Garrick's heavy body. His erection pressed into his stomach and he straightened his legs out.

Garrick promptly hooked his feet over Callum's ankles, pinning him down and kept grinding his cock inward 'till his hairy balls were pressed firmly against Callum's ass.

The heaviness of Garrick's weight above him rendered Callum helpless, but as menacing as it was knowing he could not escape the pelvic thrusts, it was strangely reassuring being anchored to him. Callum may have been giving up his ass, but in return he was receiving a man's protection. A beautiful and strong man who in this moment was shielding him from the storm of life.

"Fuck, your big." Callum moaned through Garrick's clasped fingers.

Garrick chuckled, embracing the praise. "Mmm you're a tight little fucker, aren't ya?" He whispered, his voice dripping in sex. "So fucking tight." He pulled his cock back a couple inches then rammed ahead. "Not for long though." He laughed wickedly, licking inside Callum's eardrum. He began bucking his hips, pulling his cock in and out of Callum's tautly-stretched anal lips.

It burned to buggery this whole being buggered, but

Callum waited, hoping Garrick would reach that *spot*. The place he had hit and ruptured oodles of pleasure the first time they fucked. Even with his eyes closed, Callum could see stars from the sexual energy tumbling through his entire being. Sure, it hurt, but by fucking crikey it felt great too. Garrick's heavy exhales dripped over him, watering him with the sweet smell of alcohol.

"Do you like my cock shoved in your ass?" Garrick taunted, continuing to fuck him slowly.

Callum tried to nod, wanting to give his mate the desired answer.

"What's that?" Garrick removed his hand.

"Yes. I like your cock in my ass," Callum sputtered. He tried turning his face. "Can I kiss you?"

Garrick sniggered. "You gotta earn the right to kiss my lips, slut."

Slut. The word stung like a bee. It was becoming more apparent by the second that the body impaling him may belong to his good friend, but the mind was a much darker version.

"You gonna earn my lips, slut?" Garrick jabbed Callum's ass with his cock like a full stop to his sentence.

"Ye-yes." Callum replied meekly.

"Yes, who?"

It seemed things were descending to a kinkier zone Callum had never experienced. He replied with a cliché response, hoping he was right. "Yes… *sir?*"

"That's right, slut. You're about to earn the privilege of kissing me." He squeezed hold of Callum's mouth and stuck two fingers inside. "Now suck my fingers just like you sucked my cock."

Callum wrapped his lips around the digits being fed to him, desperate to please. Garrick wriggled above him, jostling his cock side to side and expanding Callum's inexperienced hole. The prickly feel of their leg hair rubbing together gave off an energy all of its own as Garrick continued to dig his feet into Callum's ankles, keeping him locked in place and at his cock's mercy.

Garrick fired up his cock's thrusts, hammering Callum's anal cavern with greater speed and intensity, determined to wreck him. He rubbed his face against Callum's, his stubble scraping his cheek, dabbing his tongue in tease-like fashion.

Callum's mouth dripped wet moans from the river of dick eroding his cliffs of friction, the curve of Garrick's cock tunnelling him deep.

"Do you like being my bitch?" Garrick said, unashamed arrogance lacing his words. "It feels like you like it."

Callum tried answering but the fingers fucking his mouth made his words come out in jumbled slurps. He just lay taking it, his ass contracting around Garrick's member.

Garrick laughed. "I'll take that as a yes, slut" He pulled his fingers out and wrapped his arm under Callum's throat, almost putting him in a chokehold.

Fucking kiss me already! Callum craved Garrick's lips so badly, wanting the tender moment that would be a reward for the raw passion being unleashed on his fast-loosening hole. The burning of his anus was intense, and he could feel the tiny muscle becoming slack, but there was no way he was going to ask Garrick to stop doing what he was doing. In this moment Callum's only purpose was to please and impress, ride the curve of cock and take every single fucking inch.

Garrick's thrusts surged like pounding waves lashing the shoreline of Callum's body. His chest stayed pressed firmly against Callum's back, brewing up beads of sweat. With one arm still tucked under Callum's throat, he lowered his free hand down to Callum's side, dragging his fingers up and down his rib cage before slipping it underneath and grabbing hold of Callum's erection.

The firm grip with which Garrick possessed him made Callum gasp. The attention being given his pipe was delicious, prickling the hairs on his neck and making him curl his toes. Having another man's cock inside him no longer felt foreign, it was fulfilling. Every inch of Garrick's immense manhood was welcome.

Deeper, deeper, deeper. Hit that spot!

The sound of Garrick's slick skin pounding his rump crowded the room with its dull wet thudding. Garrick began to mix his steady rhythm up with brutal cock-lunges, burying his immense manhood to the hilt inside Callum's over-stretched rectum.

"You really fucking love my cock, don't you, slut?" Garrick snarled in his ear.

"Yes." *Thud.* "Mmph." *Thud.* "Sir."

"You're a fast learner. I like that," Garrick said. He bit the nape of Callum's neck, growling in a hoarse whisper. "If I was queer, I'd tie you up and fuck you for the whole night." He let go of Callum's cock and drifted his hand lower to scoop up his balls—clenching them.

"Uh…uh.." Callum's voice petered out from the frisky grope of his nuts. He felt his breath tumble out of him. He bit his lip, trying to regain hold of his senses. "Would you like fucking me all night, sir?"

Garrick slowed his fucking down 'till his dick stopped moving, remaining pressed deep inside. He began tickling Callum's squished balls. "Are you offering?" He flipped the question back to Callum, showing no sign of confirming any interest of his own.

Callum was about to say yes but Garrick jerked suddenly, his cock throbbing inside. "Fuck it," he muttered angrily. He pushed himself up, frantically pulling his cock out, creating a vacuum inside Callum's pit

Garrick ripped the condom off his dick, hurling it across the room.

Callum went to roll over; his ass feeling a strange emptiness from no longer being filled to the brim with his mate's massive organ.

"Stay the fuck down, slut." Garrick groaned loudly and shoved his cock back to Callum's raw hole.

Callum flinched and shuddered and gasped.

Garrick's prick shot scorching wetness over the surface of his battered hole. It just kept coming and coming 'till it was pooling and dribbling down his crack, leaking between his spread thighs. Callum lay frozen, shocked by the premature release.

My ass made you cum!

"Fuck that was intense," Garrick panted, trying to catch his breath. "Didn't realise I was so fucking close." He poked Callum's hole, swivelling his finger in the sexy mess, pushing some of it inside. He flopped down on the bed, laying on his back. He turned his face and smiled at Callum who was still face down. "That was fucking hot." The grin on his face was so beautiful, it was a beaming smile that seemed sincere.

Callum pressed his hands into the mattress, raising his body up and lay on his side. His cock jutted out firm and hard. He looked down at Garrick's naked body. His dick was still twitching as it slowly deflated, spunk trickling out the tip.

Garrick could see the way he was eyeing up his dick. "Suck it clean for me." He gave a flirty wink. "It's part of your job."

Callum shuffled down and lowered his face to his mate's sticky cock. He slurped up the remnants of cum and sucked gently over the tip. Garrick shuddered, sensitive to the touch. Callum swivelled his tongue over the slit, gathering every single drop of seed he could muster. When he was done, he pulled his mouth off and swallowed the residue he'd collected. He looked back at Garrick who lay back with his arms tucked behind his head like a pillow.

"So did you have fun?" Garrick asked, raising his eyebrows.

Callum nodded, smiling.

"You're still fully loaded." Garrick pointed at Callum's cock which stuck out hard and erect.

"Ha yeah…" Callum wiped his face, hoping to hide the blush colouring his face. "I guess I'll have to sort that out later."

"Don't be stupid." Garrick said.

"What?"

Instead of answering, Garrick sat up, grabbed Callum's shoulder and yanked him down on the bed so they were laying beside each other.

"What are you doing?" Callum asked, puzzled.

"Giving you your reward." Garrick smiled. He placed his lips to Callum's mouth and slipped his tongue in. The sweet taste of booze tingled Callum's taste buds. Garrick ruffled his hair affectionately as he kissed him deep and sensually.

It was exactly what Callum had wanted. The tender moment. An oscillating shiver tapped his spine. He was so wrapped up in his reward that he didn't notice Garrick slip a hand down and grab hold of his burning cock and begin to tug him off.

Garrick started slow, gradually getting faster and faster. His furled fingers enclosed Callum's dick which ached for release. Within seconds he cried out a girly noise that got lost inside Garrick's mouth. His prick shot out a heavy white load of cum splattering over the black sheets and Garrick's legs.

Callum felt his body shake and tremble like an autumn leaf, a breeze whispering over his body.

Garrick retrieved his tongue, giving Callum a light nip on the bottom lip.

Softly, they stared at each other with relieved smiles. The weirdness of the power struggle between them was gone and all that was left was pure and beautiful. It didn't feel wrong. This felt nothing but right. Callum didn't know how to convey such blissful feelings. It was almost like he was flying. The least he could do though was show gratitude for being given these wings of love. "That was amazing. Thank you." Callum smiled adoringly at his best mate, expecting a simple and equally adorable response.

His expectation wasn't met.

"So tell me," Garrick said. "How does it feel to be the newest member of my collection?"

Callum cringed. His wings were snapped and he swiftly fell back to earth.

CHAPTER FIFTEEN

Callum awoke, gasping for breath, feeling like he was still falling. He clutched his chest to make sure he was still alive. His alarm clock nightmare had taken place. He took a deep breath, trying to calm himself down. The crisp thin sheet wrapping his body was wet and clammy, he had sweated up a storm again. He rolled over in his large bed—all too big and lonely for one person—and looked towards the window. The morning was still locked in darkness like a brewing pot of black coffee. Outside the pitter patter of rain drummed atop the tin roof of his house. The pacifying sound almost sent him back to sleep.

It was horrid to think that he would have to crawl out of bed and drag his tired body to work. He didn't want to go to work today, he just wanted to hide away from the world and not face anything. Last night had changed him. His perspective of the world and who he was in it had shifted. He knew it seemed dramatic but this was how he felt. He had been curious and stupid to try stuff again with Garrick… just to answer a few things. And boy did he get his answers. Answers in the form of a rude and dismissive fuck. His tummy went topsy-turvy.

"I'm into him," Callum whispered like a defeated soldier. "Him…"

Him. It felt weird to say. It was a him he was hung up on, not a her. Even the word sounded more masculine than the softer sounding her. "Him." It had a depth to it that vibrated his voice box.

He couldn't deny it now. He had enjoyed the first night enough to go back for seconds, and even though the second session was a strange almost-kinky pity fuck, Callum still fucking loved it. He loved Garrick fucking him. He loved everything about it. The rawness. The sensuality. The dark-haired womanizer had ravished his hole, claiming Callum entirely. Laying naked in his sweat-drenched sheets, he could still feel the echo of Garrick's cock inside his sodomized ass.

Garrick was the first person since Misty that Callum had slept with more than once. The rather brief trickle of women he had been with in the initial months of friendship with Garrick had all been flings. Easy pickings designed to relieve his right hand from the lonely duty of masturbation. His self-pleasuring ritual was simple and repetitive. A wank in the shower in the morning and usually one in bed in the evening if he wasn't too knackered after a long day at work.

Against his body's wishes, Callum hauled hiss ass out of bed and wandered naked to the bathroom to get showered. Once the room was misted with warm air, he climbed inside the shower box and rest his head against the wall, letting the warmth of water trickle down his back.

He hadn't gotten anywhere near enough sleep after last night. The trip to Garrick's had ended rather abruptly after they had both lost their lollies and lay naked together on the bed. Ideally, Callum would have stayed over, sharing a bed with Garrick after sharing their sex. But following Garrick's crass question of asking if he enjoyed being the newest member of the "collection" Callum had bailed rather smartly. After a muted laugh, avoiding answering the question, he had got up off the bed and gone to the lounge and put his clothes back on and had gone straight home.

It took him hours to fall asleep, trying to shake the thoughts ruminating in his head. *What does this mean? Will we do it again? Am I gay now?* It seemed fucked-up that doing something again to answer questions had only left him even more questions.

When he had finally woken up thanks to the shower, Callum climbed out, towelled himself dry and went to get ready for work. As he raced around his bedroom looking for his work clothes, he got lost in a day dream of wondering how it would be waking up in Garrick's bedroom every morning, finding his mate asleep beside him. The notion was sweet and innocent compared to the fun they had shared. He imagined the benefit of being able to share clothes with his pal.

I wonder if we are the same size for shirts and pants?

He knew this was a stupid fantasy. He couldn't date a man. Besides, Garrick's reaction after they'd finished fucking made it very clear that all he saw Callum as was a convenient place to put his cock. And Garrick's cock had been many places.

Fuck my life. I let him make me a fucking statistic.

When Callum looked outside his window, the rain appeared to have stopped. Spring in New Zealand was marred with changeable behaviour. It was like Mother Nature was permanently pissed this time of the year. He contemplated driving into town but forced himself not to be lazy. He grabbed his raincoat just in case of another downpour and marched out the door. It didn't take long for him to regret his non-lazy decision. The grey clouds above may have stopped emptying with rain but the puddles were deceptively deep on the ground. As Callum strolled along, his toes began to squish with water filling his sneakers.

Great now I am gonna have wet cold feet all bloody day!

Coming onto the main street, still cursing for not wearing better footwear, Callum got a fright when he looked up and saw another poster glued to the lamppost. He grimaced expecting to see his sister's nude picture again, but to his relief it was an advert for the upcoming Labour Weekend celebrations.

LABOUR WEEKEND CELEBRATION
Town fair and the annual Tasman Height's Fun Run!

Labour Weekend was the biggest event on Tasman Height's social calendar. It signalled a rather premature start of summer when all the locals would equally love and hate the abundance of out-of-towners beginning to come to town for their holidays and cramp the village's chilled style. Still, without these tourists, business owners like Callum would be out of pocket and it was the ridiculous spending habits of these imports that kept a roof over many local's heads.

The fun run was the pinnacle event of the weekend holiday celebration. They may have called it a *fun run* but it was anything but fun. It was a gut-wrenching five kilometre run around the harbour that led onto a stretch of mud-filled trenches you had to trudge through before swimming up Rapanui estuary where spectators would stand on the footbridge and throw paint and flour over you as you swam under what was the finish line—you just prayed that no fucking idiots slipped through safety checks and dropped stones or hard-boiled eggs.

Callum and Garrick usually competed every year as part of their friendly rivalry. Each time Garrick had beat him and come in the top five racers overall, whereas Callum was usually further behind in the middle of the pack—a position his mother would call "a very good average."

Callum wasn't sure if he would compete this year. The café was barely solvent and he wasn't sure he could afford to pay for an extra staff member to cover his shift just to go play in mud like some kid at kindergarten. Besides, he didn't need to be losing any more of his pride to Garrick who would no doubt crow about his "spectacular victory" for weeks on end.

What kind of punishment would he expect if he won that big race?

Callum quickly wiped the smile from his face when he realised he was getting excited about such degrading prospects. *What the fuck is wrong with me.* He needed to get Garrick out of his head. He couldn't possibly expect Garrick to give him some sort of tender romance. That wasn't in the guy's nature. *He said himself he only fucked me out of some sort of pity.*

Nothing good could come from pursuing him. Besides, he didn't need to get preoccupied with falling for someone he couldn't have—especially when that person came equipped with a cock. He could only imagine how well that would be received. The whole town would have a bloody field day to find out the once cool kid of Tasman Heights High had gone gay. He cringed internally at the thought of how much he would get mocked by locals.

Growing up he had flung the word *faggot* around generously at his mates jokingly and they had all taken great delight in hurling it at David Williams in their final year of school. Callum wondered if David held a grudge against them all for the cruel abuse he had received. With his own same-sex feelings bubbling beneath the surface, Callum felt especially awful for the way he had treated the poor kid. Lost in memories of guilt, Callum began to unlock the door to the café. As he let himself inside he had a jolt of panic when he realised he had forgotten something.

I didn't kiss Misty good morning.

For the first time in two years he had forgotten to kiss the photo of his one and only beside his bed. Instead it was Garrick who had been the one to get his loving affectionate thoughts.

Oh dear…

CHAPTER SIXTEEN

Callum took his seat at the table waiting for his sister to dish him up his reward meal for pulling all her scandalous photos down. Julie wasn't much of a cook and judging by the way Graham sat at the table with a cautious face, Callum suspected that the household was probably more use to takeout or microwave meals than a roast chicken and vegetable dish.

"Only a few more minutes away," Julie hollered from the kitchen before hissing, "Ough fuck that's hot!"

"Did you need some help in there, Nigella?" Callum asked, chuckling.

"No. I have it under control. I just burnt my hand on the oven door."

Callum sniggered while Graham's mouth curled into a worried line.

"Did you want me to get some ice, babe?" Graham called out.

"Nar, I'm okay, babe," Julie returned. "Just do me a favour and hit my idiot brother for laughing at my pain."

Babe. Callum missed that word. He missed having someone to call him babe and he missed having someone to call it. Such a simple word to most, but when uttered between lovers it had its own meaning. It showed a bond—a closeness and language that was a couple's own.

"Hey, boss," said a deep, familiar voice.

Callum spun 'round in his seat and saw Nicky entering the lounge. "Hey, how's my star employee?"

Nicky smiled. "I'm good thanks." He took a seat at the table opposite Callum.

"How's your day off been?" Callum asked.

"Okay," the boy replied without an ounce of

excitement.

"Just okay?" Callum questioned. "You didn't get out and get up to no good then?"

"I imagine he spent all day in his lair playing computer games," Graham answered for his son, or as Julie called Nicky in private; "Graham's mini me."

Nicky and his dad shared the same brown hair and sleepy hazel eyes. Both had pleasant faces without being striking. And aside from Graham being more aged in the face and possessing broader shoulders and fuller chest, the two really were easy to pick as father and son, even down to the same manly voice and relaxed posture.

"Are you a gamer?" Callum asked, trying to start a conversation. At work they barely talked other than Nicky saying "Yes, boss" to any chore he was given.

"Sort of" Nicky mumbled. He tugged at his shirt with his slim fingers, staring down at his chest.

"You don't have to keep counting them, Nicky. I'm sure their still there." Graham said with a warm smile.

"Counting what?" Callum asked, confused.

"His chest hairs," Graham joked.

"Nar, I wasn't counting that." Nicky blushed, giving away the fact he probably was doing exactly what his father just said.

"Enjoy it while you can," Julie's voice interrupted. "One day you'll be like your father and have too many to count." She appeared in the dining room, carrying a bowl of roast vegetables and put them on the centre of the table. She brushed Graham's shoulder affectionately. "I must say I had no idea I'd end up dating Chewbacca."

"Pfft," Graham laughed. "I think that may be a gross exaggeration, babe."

"I'm just saying both sides of you are so hairy that when we're in bed I never know if I am hugging you from the front or behind." She smiled at Callum, letting him know she was just teasing her man.

Callum spotted Nicky frowning, displeased by the intimate comment. Anything remotely to do with a parent's sex life was probably not something a son wanted to hear.

Graham reached out tickling Julie's sides, sending her giggling back into the kitchen. The pair were definitely still loved-up and in the happy phase of the relationship. Callum suspected Graham couldn't believe his luck to have scored such a pretty girlfriend. Still, he was a good man and Callum was grateful to him for helping his sister settle down.

Graham settled his smile down and turned to Callum with a serious expression. "Did Julie tell you about what happened today?"

Julie suddenly reappeared in the dining room looking flustered. "Someone slashed my car tyres."

"They what?" Callum spat out.

"Yeah. At work today... someone slashed my tyres in the carpark."

"Oh my god. Why?" Callum asked.

Julie shrugged her shoulders.

"Do you think it's the same person who—" Callum started. Julie shot him a stern look that told him to shut his mouth. She mustn't have told Graham about the photo incident.

"The same person who?" Graham stared at Callum waiting for the answer.

"The same person who..." Callum let the words dangle a little too long, unsure what lie to invent.

"The same person who went slashing tyres up the main street yesterday," Julie lied for him. She glared at Callum, urging him to back her up.

"Yeah. Someone slashed some poor bugger's car tyres outside work yesterday." Callum bit his lip, nodding.

"Did they?" Nicky blurted. "I never saw."

Callum's stomach somersaulted, forgetting about Nicky working yesterday. "Yeah... it happened after you and Jess had gone home when it was just me there on my own."

Nicky nodded slowly, surprised by the tale.

"Hmm. That is shocking. Some phantom going around town slashing."

Julie and Callum giggled by Graham's innocent choice

of words.

"Better that than a phantom crapper," Julie said light-heartedly.

Graham didn't laugh. "I can't see how you think someone costing us and other innocent people hundreds of dollars is at all funny." The tone in the voice gave away the man was a parent. Callum wondered how often Nicky had heard his father use that nagging voice.

Callum looked up at his sister. "Yes. It isn't good."

Julie gave him a guilty look. "Okay time to get this chicken out. Hope you're hungry." On those fluffy words, she darted out of sight.

∞

"Why didn't you bloody tell me about your tyres being slashed," Callum whispered heatedly to his sister. They were outside on the back porch, where Julie was having her after dinner cigarette. A habit Graham did not approve of so he sat inside watching tele with Nicky in the lounge.

"I didn't want you to worry." She inhaled deeply on the cancer stick in her hand.

"I'm your brother. That's my job."

Julie rolled her eyes. "I have Graham to do that so you needn't worry, Callum."

"You being with Graham doesn't take away any of my responsibility." Callum stepped back to avoid a plume of smoke Julie exhaled. "And even if it did, it's not like you have told him the truth for him to worry about it."

Julie shook her head. "There isn't anything to worry about."

"Really? So someone plasters nude pictures of you all down the main street and then slashes your tyres," Callum said. "That tells me there is something to worry about."

"Keep your voice down," Julie snapped, flicking her eyes towards inside. "I don't need Graham freaking out about this for no good reason."

"But I think there is a good reason to freak out,"

Callum protested.

Julie coughed up a coy smile. "I can assure you there is not."

"Why?"

"I have a sneaky suspicion who it is." Julie nibbled on her lip.

"Who?"

"I can't say."

"For fuck sake, Julie, just tell me."

"Calm your farm, it's no one you know." She paused before taking a deep breath. "Look, I suspect it's a girl from work who went for the same promotion as me and missed out. Garrick put in a good word for me and I believe that helped me get the role over her." She paused, looking behind her towards the lounge. "I don't want to say anything to Graham because I don't want him knowing about my history with a co-worker."

"Do you think he'd have an issue with that. He's a pretty relaxed guy."

"Yes, but even Graham would probably get an inferiority complex if he saw who Garrick was."

"So sleeping with your HR manager paid off in the end," Callum joked.

"Yeah, probably the only good thing to come from sleeping with the shmuck."

"Was he bad in bed?" Callum blurted without thinking. *Did he only perform good for me?* The stupid thought was wishful thinking at best.

Julie furrowed her brow. "How the hell did you get that from what I just said?"

Callum tried to hide his embarrassment and real reason for asking. "My bad."

Julie laughed. "For the record, he was... okay," she said coyly, like she was hiding some delicious surprise.

She didn't need to be coy. Callum knew how good the man was at making love. *And fucking like a heathen.*

"So let me get this straight," Callum said. "You get a promotion at work—thanks to Garrick putting in a good word—and this girl posts nude photos and slashes your tyres?" He ran a hand through his hair. "Is it that cut throat at the council?"

"Apparently so."

"But how did she get the photos?"

"I lost my phone, remember?" Julie said defensively. "I'm picking that when I left my desk or something last week, she has stolen my phone out of my handbag."

"Shit," Callum muttered. "You should tell Garrick about this. See what can be done."

"I'm not telling Garrick or anyone anything," Julie said. "I spoke with the little witch today and so she knows I know it's her and I can tell she is too petrified to do anything else."

"Are you sure?"

"Yes, Callum. I am sure." Julie gave a stern stare that told her brother to back off. "Anyway, I had something I want to ask you."

"What's that?"

"What are you doing Labour Weekend?"

"I'm not entering the fun run if that's what you're asking."

"That's not what I was going to ask." Julie smiled. "I was going to ask you if you fancied coming with me for a long weekend in Fiji. Four nights staying at a five-star hotel. The tickets are super cheap at the moment and it would be great to get away for a few days—just the two of us."

Callum laughed. "Are you serious?"

"Why would I joke about that?"

"Well, you and me haven't hung out alone together longer than an hour since we shared Mum's womb. And for good reason—we always end up fighting."

"No we don't."

Callum laughed. "Do you not remember how much of a nightmare you were to live with growing up."

"Excuse me, but *you* were the nightmare. Not me." Julie shot him a mischievous grin. "Anyway, we're grownups now. I think I can put up with your bullshit for five days if I tried."

"Ha. It would be me putting up with your bullshit," Callum said, nudging his sister with his elbow.

"Well… what do you think?"

"Labour Weekend is only two weeks away… it's not much notice and it's not like I can afford it."

"It would be my treat," Julie said warmly.

"How can you afford it?"

"Gee thanks for the lovely praise, Callum." Julie laughed. "I can afford it because I had the good sense to get engaged to a wealthy man. Maybe you should consider doing the same." Her eyes twinkled with cheek.

"Piss off," Callum fired back.

"Sorry, I meant find a wealthy woman." She tapped his arm. "Come on. Come to Fiji with me. Graham has said it's a good idea. That way him and Nicky can do some father son bonding for his birthday and you and me can soak up the sun for a bit."

"Is it Nicky's birthday soon?"

Julie nodded. "Yep. He turns eighteen on the same day as the fun run. I think him and Graham are going to compete together. It would be hilarious to watch them both, but I'd rather go soak up the sun with my brother on a pacific island."

"But we already live on a pacific island," Callum teased.

"A warmer one." She pleaded with her eyes. "I could do with a break from playing the third wheel for a while."

Callum was taken aback by his sister's tone. "What do you mean third wheel?"

"Haven't you noticed how Nicky is always around? He never gives me a chance to be alone with Graham. It's so frustrating."

Callum tried not to laugh. His sister was the one sounding like a teenager. "Nicky's all good. He just likes being around his dad. What's wrong with that?"

Julie shook her head, defeated. "Nothing, I guess. I just wish he wasn't around *quite* so much."

Callum widened his eyes.

"Yes. I know how bad that sounds but I just... I can't put my finger on it," Julie said. I just feel like he does it on purpose. You know he nearly refused taking the unit. He wanted a room inside the house. What teen would not want their own self-contained unit... seriously?"

"Maybe he isn't as devious as you were at that age, sneaking your boyfriends inside the house."

"Very funny," Julie replied sarcastically. "Anyway. How about it? You and me, kicking it back in Fiji."

Callum wished he could accept the generous offer, but it didn't feel right. He had never taken a dime from his sister, let alone an all-expenses paid holiday. "I can't."

"Don't be a proud fool, Callum," Julie said. "You deserve a bit of generosity after all the shit you've done for me through the years."

Callum looked down at his feet, scuffing his shoe on the patio. "It's not just that." He looked up and met his sister's intense gaze. "I need to be here to run the café."

"Just get Mum in to run it for a few days. She is more than capable."

"No. It's my responsibility and I don't want anyone else in there until I have it back to how it should be running. And you know Labour Weekend will make or break me."

Julie let out a frustrated sigh. "I really wish you'd just stop being stubborn and come with me."

"You should go with Mum. She would enjoy the break away from Dad and his stamp collection," Callum joked. He saw how annoyed Julie was looking with him for turning the holiday down. "Why are you so adamant on me coming with you all of a sudden. You've never wanted us to go away together before."

"No reason," Julie said in a shrill voice. "It just felt like the right thing to do. But if you're too much of a martyr to have a good time then that's your problem" She threw her cigarette away and in a snotty voice asked, "Shall we go inside now?"

"Sure," Callum said, stretching his arms out wide.

"But can you help me carry this cross on my back." He winced, feigning pain.

Julie whacked his shoulder, giving into laughter. "Please don't pull that face ever again."

Callum lowered his arms, smiling. "Why?"

"You look like someone just shoved their cock in your ass."

Callum's stomach knotted. *Trust me. That isn't the face I pull.*

CHAPTER SEVENTEEN

Callum was sat at home on the couch in just a pair of shorts while he waited for his clothes in the dryer. Not just any clothes but his best outfit that rocked a mix of smart and casual; metallic jeans and a slim-fitting black t-shirt. He intended to look his best tonight.

He stroked his fingers back and forward across his nipples, admiring his lean, tanned torso. Even in winter his skin held onto an olive complexion many people envied. With his chin pressed down, he resembled Nicky counting stray chest hairs. Callum assumed he would have a fair few more than his teen worker but not enough to be considered a rug. Not like Garrick whose chest homed a sizable island of dark hair.

Callum's eyes drifted shut as he remembered the feel of his mate's hairy chest scratching his smooth back. It had been innately sexual and had helped add to the entire experience. Pinned beneath Garrick's manly body and being force-fed his meaty tool had been fucking hot. And after enough time to recover from the shame and degradation of what Garrick had inflicted, Callum begun to think he could do it again... *maybe*.

He opened his eyes, escaping from the saucy memory. He looked around the lounge, scoping out its tidy condition. It was the cleanest the place had been in weeks and smelled great thanks to the lavender scented candles he had lit an hour earlier. Keeping a tidy home wasn't a skill Callum excelled at, and unlike Garrick, he didn't have the luxury of affording a house keeper. Misty had always been the one to tidy up. It wasn't that he believed housework to be a woman's job; the truth was just that Callum was—and always had been—a messy shit.

However, today he had come home straight from work and gone on a cleaning blitz; scrubbing the shower and toilet, vacuuming the floors, doing the dishes and even made his bed. The reason for his sudden embracing of keeping a tidy abode?

Garrick.

To Callum's delight—and relief—Garrick was coming around for game night. It was a rare event for them to hang out in Callum's humble home, but Garrick had turned up unexpectedly at the café and said to expect him this evening just after eight.

Since being added to Garrick's collection, Callum had become very worried that their friendship had possibly ended. He had not received a single phone call or text since giving his ass up a second time, so when Garrick walked into the café earlier today, acting like nothing was out of the ordinary, Callum had felt a rush of relief flood his body. Callum would have been more relieved had the impromptu visit to the café not happened when and how it did, creating a situation that had been more than a touch awkward.

Still, Garrick's parting words from the unexpected visit had planted a seed of hope in Callum's horny mind. A seed he hoped would grow every bit as big and thick as Garrick's cock.

∞

Callum sat talking with Sherry in the café, going over her dish wish list for Mandy's birthday. Her selection was nothing too fancy, and luckily enough the items would be cheap to order. If he worked alone then Callum stood to make a pretty penny.

"Just make sure nothing is too spicy. Mandy goes bonkers about anything too hot," Sherry said.

"Okay," Callum mumbled, looking over the list.

"Yes, the only spice she likes is ginger."

Callum laughed, looking up at Sherry who stroked her

gorgeous red hair. "Yes, if I were her that's all I'd ever eat." He quickly apologised, "Sorry. That wasn't meant to come out quite so... vulgar."

Sherry giggled. "Settle down, Callum. It's okay. You do know lesbians can handle a dirty joke like everybody else."

"Phew. Good to know." He went back to reading the list.

Sherry suddenly ripped the sheet away, hiding it under the table. Callum went to question what the hell she was doing but all she did was whisper, "Go with the flow."

With a look of confusion, he spun around to find Garrick approaching their table, dressed in his work attire of white collared shirt and crisp-looking grey trousers. He looked incredible as always and somehow made it look effortless.

"I wondered why you left for lunch early," Garrick said loudly, taking a seat down at the table with them. Immediately his musky cologne wormed its way up Callum's nostrils, making him woozy with lust.

"Naughty me, ducking out ten minutes early," Sherry said. "Nothing gets past you, Mr Masters."

Garrick smiled facetiously. "Of course not. I'm HR. That's my job."

Sherry chuckled. "It's okay. I was actually about to head back now anyway. I was just coming to ask Callum if we were still on for Saturday."

"What's happening Saturday?" Garrick asked, confused.

"If you must know," Sherry purred, "Callum is taking me out for dinner."

"I am?" Callum blurted. Sherry kicked his shin under the table. "Uh yeah... well I am making you dinner I mean... for... for our date."

Sherry giggled. "Out or in. It's all good with me. Just make sure the food is as tasty as you." She flicked Garrick a smug smile then stood up. "Okay. I better get back to work before I get dobbed in for being late. Call me tomorrow about dinner, okay?"

"Uh… yeah. Sure," Callum spluttered. He watched Garrick's shocked brown eyes follow Sherry leave the store.

Garrick's posture stiffened. "Does she actually dig you?"

Callum didn't like the way Garrick had said that. "Why wouldn't she?"

"Because you aren't me." He smiled back arrogantly.

"Gee. Maybe this is one time I win." Callum saw how annoyed Garrick appeared, he felt guilty and was about to tell him the truth but got cut off by his cocky pal.

"Nar, man. I can tell she's after me. She's just using you to try and get me worked up."

"Really," Callum replied sarcastically.

"Yep. She knows that the best way to win me over is by making me jealous by pretending to be into my best mate."

Normally Garrick's arrogance and cocky assumptions didn't bother Callum, but for some reason he found Garrick's indifference to him being a threat very hurtful. "Yet it's me going on a date with her on Saturday—not you." Callum arched his eyebrows, enjoying the cheap shot. Suddenly, Sherry's plan didn't feel so nasty.

"Well, I guess we will find out. It's all fair in love and war 'till the pants are down." He waggled his eyebrows.

"True," Callum mumbled.

"Anyway, I was just dropping in to see what the plan is for game night."

"It's on?" Callum asked cautiously.

Garrick frowned, looking completely surprised by Callum's response. "Yeah. It's Thursday. Why wouldn't it be?"

Callum hesitated a little too long. "No reason."

"I thought tonight maybe we could do it at your place. Have a change of scene, aye? Give you home court advantage for once."

"Yeah, sure."

"Okay. All good if I drop by after eight."

"What game?" Callum asked just as Garrick was

standing up.

Garrick stared down at him, biting his lip. "You choose." He went to walk away like nothing was different between them. Just as he got to the door, he spun 'round and called out, "But remember, Callum, the loser *takes* it all." With a salacious wink, he walked off as arrogantly as he had arrived.

Callum sat at the table, his face burning red from the loud declaration. He looked at the counter and saw Jess and Nicky talking, none the wiser to the potentially gay comment Garrick had fired out loud. He took a deep breath. *I better make sure I win.*

∞

Callum had just got changed into his freshly dried outfit when the door sounded with three cheerful knocks. He smiled to himself and hopped down the hallway on one leg, trying to put his last sock on. As much as Garrick's arrogance had annoyed him at the café, he couldn't deny that his mate deserved to be arrogant. Callum had always known how handsome his friend was, any guy—gay or straight—could see Garrick Masters was a fine specimen. But Callum could more than see it now. He could sense and taste it thanks to the intimacy they'd shared. An intimacy that made him long to be touched by the city slicker's magic hands one more time.

Maybe tonight he will stay over if I ask him nicely?

The thought was wonderful. If things went the way they had at Garrick's house, then they would surely end up exploring this queer path a bit more. With game night being at his own house, maybe Garrick would be too drunk to drive home? Maybe they could actually make love together in bed? If he did sleep over, Callum could feel the closeness and warmth of his conqueror's naked body beside him. The mere thought made his cock pulse with the buzz of horny hope.

Callum managed to slip the sock over his foot just before he reached the door. "Game night begins. Prepare to get your ass kicked, Mr Masters," he said with a happy laugh, pulling the door open.

As soon as he opened the door, Callum knew right away there would be no exploratory fun tonight. He stared ahead with a dropped jaw, shocked at what was before him.

CHAPTER EIGHTEEN

Past and present stood side by side at his front door. Garrick Masters and Tim Chadwick.

"What the..." Callum said, trailing off. He couldn't believe his eyes. "Tim?"

"The one and fucking only, brother." Tim was beaming with a huge smile.

Callum stepped aside, letting his friends walk inside out of the cold.

Tim turned around and extended his hand for a shake. "How the fuck are ya, bro?"

"I'm... I'm good," Callum muttered, still in shock by the bizarre reunion. He put his hand out for the shake, but Tim reeled him in for a bear hug.

"Fuck. It's so good to see you again," Tim said, patting him hard on the back.

Callum stepped back from the hefty hug, looking his best mate up and down. He couldn't believe he was seeing Tim for the first time in nearly three years. He looked just the same; tall, slim, with cheeky hazel eyes and a boyish face framed by shaggy brown hair. He was wearing a baggy white t-shirt and dirty denim jeans. The casual look was accompanied by a light shade of stubble on his face.

"When did you get back in town?" Callum asked.

"I got back yesterday, bro. I'm here for a few weeks doing the family thing," Tim said, quickly adding, "And to see you of course."

"Good stuff," Callum said, he looked at Garrick with confused eyes. "I didn't know you two knew each other."

"We don't." Tim laughed. "After I got back last night I pretty much hit the hay at the olds then today when I ventured out to the grocery store I bumped into this player and he asked if I was Tim—Callum's mate—and when I said yes, G star here told me about your game night and suggested I come along and surprise you." Tim nodded, smiling. "Like… I was planning on coming to see you tonight anyway but this sounded a better idea."

"You sure have surprised me." Callum nodded along to the unbelievable coincidence. He stared at Garrick. "But how did you recognise Tim?"

"It's called photographs, Callum." Garrick sniggered. "You have a few pics of this tall prick in your lounge remember?" He laughed. "Of course I know what your *best mate* looks like."

Best mate. He's jealous!

"True," Callum replied, still slightly dumbstruck.

"Oi watch who you're calling a tall prick, bro," Tim said, laughing. He slapped Garrick on the shoulder and looked at Callum. "I'm glad you found yaself a replacement after I left. Maybe not as fun as me but he seems okay."

"He sure did find a replacement. And he traded up while he was at it."

"Yeah, yeah," Tim chuckled.

"Yep. I give Callum here things you never dreamed of," Garrick said, winking.

Tim found this hilarious, bursting out in laughter again, unfazed by what Callum suspected wasn't an innocent joke. "Good shit," Tim said, looking around the kitchen. "Place looks pretty similar to when I was last here. I thought you would have painted over the bright fucking walls by now."

Callum ran a hand through his hair. "Yeah, that's the plan. But when Misty left, the money walked out with her." He smiled, trying to downplay how depressing being broke was. Hoping it would also cover the fact he wouldn't have changed a single thing in the house anyway.

Tim nodded solemnly. "Yeah. That's stink, bro. I wish I could have come up and seen ya. I know how cut up you were, but fucking money was my problem too. This is the first time I've had any spare cash to come home." He rubbed

Callum's shoulder.

"That's all good, mate." Callum nodded. Tim didn't have to tell him about the limitations money put on life. He knew them all too well. Still, he had secretly harboured a slight resentment that Tim hadn't tried harder to make a visit when Misty left him. It was only when he became mates with Garrick that he had let that sour point go.

"Onwards and upwards like they say." Tim grinned at him.

"Yep. Onwards and upwards," Callum agreed.

"Do you have enough booze for all three of us to get hammered tonight?" Garrick asked, casting Callum a quick glance pointing at the fridge.

"Yeah, should do," Callum answered. "I have more in the pantry but the chilled ones are in there."

Garrick went and opened the fridge and pulled out two RTD bottles of bourbon.

"So what's this game night all about then lads?" Tim asked.

Garrick strode over and handed Tim one of the bottles. "Well, we usually play cards and have a wee gamble where the winner—usually me—gets the winnings and the loser gets to take shit for not being good enough."

Tim smiled. "I better not lose too much. I don't wanna lose my money and take too much shit."

Garrick took a mouthful of his drink, eyeing Callum discretely. "Yeah. Gotta be careful 'round here, Tim. The loser takes it all."

∞

Instead of getting straight into playing a round of cards, Callum had led his friends into the lounge where they sat and yakked, waffling loads of shit. Garrick sat mostly in silence, letting Tim and Callum catch up on the past three years. After the initial awkwardness of Garrick arriving with Tim, Callum had taken a while to adjust to the dynamic. He hadn't been prepared to be hosting both friends. He had planned ahead for the possibility of some frisky fun, going out and buying a pack of condoms when picking up the alcohol for tonight. Now it was obvious that his newly purchased rubbers would stay in the packet unused.

Fucking typical. It seemed just Callum's luck to get his hopes up for something to only have them dashed. But the more Callum got lost going down memory lane with Tim, he began to wonder if it was for the best. Fucking your mate wasn't the done thing. The kind of romance Callum had craved was forbidden. You don't screw the crew. And maybe if they stopped now they could go back to some sort of normalcy, pretend it was all a dream.

Tim was his usual colourful self, sharing comical stories of his new life in Christchurch. He used lively body language as he re-enacted some of his wild nights out and work shenanigans. Even with the city still recovering, Tim insisted the place had a good spirit and that there was tonnes of fun to be had.

As well as being the biggest joker of the small party, Tim was also the biggest drinker. While Callum and Garrick paced themselves on the drinks, Tim guzzled them down like his mouth was on fire. He was already swaying in his seat when he asked if Callum and Garrick fancied joining him outside for a spliff.

Callum shook his head. "No thanks. None for me."

"What about you, G star?" Tim waved the fat joint in his hand. "Fancy joining me, bro?"

Garrick shook his head to dismiss the idea. "I'm all good, thanks."

Tim got to his feet, staggering towards the lounge ranch slider door. His lanky limbs wobbled as he heaved it open, nearly losing his balance.

Callum laughed at his tall pal nearly arsing over but Tim regathered his balance and slurred, "I don't go down that easily." He giggled and went outside, shutting the door behind him.

It was the first time of the night that Callum and Garrick had a proper moment alone.

"I can't believe you two banged into each other like that," Callum said. He took a swig on his drink. "It's such a small world."

"Sure is," Garrick said, making fierce eye contact. "So when's your date night with Sherry?" His voice sharp and accusing.

"Saturday," Callum answered, going along with the fictitious date, hoping to make his pal jealous.

"True," Garrick grunted. "So will you fuck her?"

"Excuse me?"

"I said. Will. You. Fuck. Her?"

Callum released a nervous laugh. "None of your business."

"Yeah. Sorry." Garrick shot over a smarmy smile. "You know she's on my hit list, right?"

Callum rolled his eyes.

"It's okay," Garrick said. "I'm not saying you can't go there."

"Okay." Callum nodded. He didn't like lying to Garrick but it felt good to see him getting a bit hot under the collar from having competition.

"I spose you'll probably think of me while you fuck her."

Callum nearly spat his drink out. "What?"

"Oh, come on, Callum. I know it's me you'd rather spend a night with."

"As if."

"Really? Even though twice now I've gone inside your ass balls-deep and both times you've been fucking gagging for it."

Callum pointed with his eyes towards outside where Tim was. "Keep your voice down. Tim might hear you."

"He won't hear shit. The dude is already pissed and halfway to being stoned."

Garrick was probably right, but it didn't make Callum anymore comfortable to have this sort of conversation.

"Anyway, I see you're not denying it," Garrick said.

"Denying what?"

"That you loved me fucking you." Garrick smiled, showing off his straight white teeth.

Fucking cocky shit. Callum resisted the urge to hurl a curse word across the room.

"It's not like you could deny it," Garrick added. "I mean, look at you!"

"What are you on about?"

"Look at what you're wearing. You don't think I know that you got dressed up especially just for me. That you didn't put on your sexiest cologne for me to smell, hoping it'd make me wanna fool around again?"

Callum flinched internally. How the fuck could Garrick know these things? The only respite was that at least he called the cologne sexy. "You're talking shit," Callum flung back in defence. He slugged back on his bottle, swallowing his shame.

Even though they had fucked twice now—and Callum knew beyond a doubt he craved a third time—Garrick didn't make it easy to open up to him. It was like the guy got a thrill out of making Callum squirm, trying to make him feel ashamed and inferior.

"Come on, Callum." Garrick ran a hand through his dark hair. "We both know you want a piece of this." He dropped his hand to his crotch, groping himself. "Why deny yourself what it is you want?"

"Are you sure this isn't a case of you wanting it?" Callum stared back, looking cool and collected, denying the desperation clawing up his throat.

"Ha. Reverse psychology. Nice one." Garrick shifted in his seat, looking around the room. "Yeah. I wouldn't mind a blowjob. You're pretty good at it."

Callum felt his limbs shake with a mix of want and anger from the compliment that wasn't really a compliment.

Garrick groped his crotch again. "Come on, *slut.* Come suck me real quick."

"Fuck you," Callum muttered.

Garrick leant forward, resting his elbows on his knees, staring dead ahead. "No, Callum, I'm the one who does the fucking remember. So *fuck* you!"

The sharp response was the angriest Callum had heard Garrick before. He nibbled his lip, thinking over how to respond.

"I will give you one last chance. Apologise for being a fuckwit and I will consider letting you suck my cock again."

"How the hell am I being a fuckwit?"

"Because you are pissing me about, trying to be a cock tease, and lying about what it is you want."

"Am I now?" Callum shook his head. "Gee, I am so sorry, Garrick, for *pissing you about*." The sarcasm was thick and loud.

"Well, if you wanna play silly games, Callum, then I guess I will just have to go find someone else to fuck tonight."

You what! It was like Garrick had just fired a poisoned arrow straight into his heart.

Garrick suddenly stood up, walking briskly across the room and came and stood right in front of him. For a brief moment, Callum thought Garrick was about to hit him, but instead, he extended a hand and delicately brushed the side of his face.

A shiver of lust warbled through Callum's system. Garrick's hand carried a warmth and sexual energy that was frying his skin. It was all it took to make him crumble and surrender. He leant forward and kissed the crotch of Garrick's jeans, burying any doubt about his attraction. "You're so fucking hot," he whispered.

"I like to think so," Garrick said arrogantly. He stroked Callum's cheek with his thumb. "If you do as your told then I'll give you what you want."

"What I want?" Callum asked in a brittle voice, waiting to be told what his own want was.

"I'll spend the night with you," Garrick said, continuing to stroke the side of his face.

Callum gulped. It was as if Garrick had a sexual sixth sense. That was what he wanted. A night where they were together, in bed, side by side. "And I just have to do what I'm told?"

Garrick lowered himself, hovering his body in an almost-crouching position so they were to face. "Yes. If you do *everything* you're told to, then I will stay the night." He hitched his eyebrows up. "If you take a risk for once in your life—and I mean a *real* fucking risk—then you might find you just get what it is you want."

Being called out for his sensible streak was hurtful. It was the same insult Misty had flung at him the day she walked out, slamming the door behind her. Garrick's comment however, felt like he was opening a door... a door which Callum had to be brave enough to walk through.

"It's all in your hands now," Garrick whispered. "Are you man enough?"

Callum nodded, despite his reservations. He wasn't sure if it was the gravelly tone or the lecherous sneer spreading on Garrick's lips, but something told him to be weary. The night was perfectly still outside but that didn't mean a storm wasn't brewing inside the house.

CHAPTER NINETEEN

Garrick had only just walked away from stroking Callum's face and sat back down when Tim rattled the door open, returning inside. He stumbled his way back to the couch, plonking down beside Garrick. He slumped onto the couch, spreading his long legs wide, showing just how chilled out the joint had made him.

"Did that hit the spot for ya?" Garrick asked, tapping Tim on the arm.

"Suuure did," Tim slurred, smiling. "I've got another for later if you lads fancy sharing."

Garrick and Callum both shook their heads.

Callum stared over at the clock. He fought back an involuntary yawn that came on in reaction to seeing it was just after ten o'clock. Normally he would be in bed by now if he didn't have company. He knew he should be more excited about catching up with Tim but Tim's unplanned presence had ruined his plans. Devious plans that involved beating Garrick in a game of cards and then cashing in his victory by making Garrick pay up the price of losing; stripped naked and bending over to be fucked. Just thinking about the shoe being on the other foot brought about a delicious feeling in his balls.

But the shoe wasn't going to be on the other foot. Garrick had made that clear. Callum was to do as he was told if he wanted a slice of him again. Still, the thought of spending a night together was wildly intoxicating. Even if he had to be subservient to get there, it would be worth it, Callum decided. He was man enough. He would take the risk. He would walk through that door.

"Grab us a couple more drinks would you, Callum." Garrick pointed towards the kitchen to back up his request.

Callum looked back at him with a coy expression, wondering why Garrick just didn't get up and fetch his own drink like he had been all evening.

"Gee, mate. Aren't you going to do as your *told*," Garrick said with a dose of good humour for Tim's benefit.

"Sure," Callum replied, jolting to life. He stood up and wandered to the kitchen and fetched his friends another drink each. As he bowed his head into the cool air of the refrigerator, it struck him how like Julie he was in this moment. Rushing after Garrick like he was a king.

Callum returned with two drinks and handed them over to his pals. He smiled at Garrick and went to sit back down.

"You've trained him well, I see," Tim joked.

"Like you wouldn't believe," Garrick replied, sneaking Callum a sultry look that only the pair of them knew its real meaning.

"Tell me, Tim. What was Callum here like at high school?" Garrick asked.

Tim giggled for no reason, the pot making him find anything funny. He looked across at Callum, studying him with bloodshot eyes. "Callum was Mr popular."

Garrick frowned as if flummoxed. "Really?"

"Shit, don't sound too surprised," Callum said.

"Yeah, man. All the girls wanted him." Tim giggled. "Even our token shirt-lifter David Williams wanted a piece of Callum."

Garrick focused his attention on Callum. "David Williams? Doesn't his family run the supermarket?"

Callum nodded. Guilt rippled through him, remembering how mean they had been to David

"David-poofter-Williams had a big crush on Callum," Tim said. "You'd need a fucking mop to clean up all the drool on the ground every time he saw Callum playing soccer shirtless."

Garrick sipped back on his drink, keeping his eyes on Callum like he was imagining him shirtless running around a field. He put his drink down and asked, "So did you ever fool around with David?"

Tim slapped his knee bursting out with an overly loud laugh. "Good shit. Yeah, Callum, did you ever play hide the sausage with him?"

"Piss off," Callum muttered.

"Maybe David didn't meet Callum's taste in men," Garrick said.

Callum's nerves sloshed inside him. He didn't dare come back with a smart-ass reply, too worried if Garrick dropped their secret like a bomb. He had no intention of Tim finding out about his newly-discovered fondness for men. Tim was a cool guy but had a big fucking mouth and could easily pass on any secrets. The way Garrick sat so comfortably, taunting Callum with his words told Callum that Garrick didn't care if people found out. Garrick was so confident and self-assured that he probably wouldn't give a shit if people found out he had fucked another man in the ass.

Tim and Garrick shared confidence as a trait, but they were very different in other ways. Garrick was more reserved than the loud Tim and while Garrick had an open mind, Tim was just a typical kiwi bloke; he loved his booze, women and sport. If he found out what Callum had done with Garrick it would not be well-received.

"How was the flight up?" Callum blurted at Tim, trying to change the topic quickly.

Tim blinked back at him, taken aback by the random question. "I didn't fly up. I drove."

"Really? That must have taken ages." Callum smiled. "And probably cost more."

"Yeah, I was gonna fly up but figured this way if I have my car with me I won't be stuck relying on the olds to transport my ass here and there the whole time."

"True." Callum nodded.

"It took two days to get here," Tim expanded, "but it was a great fucking trip. I had perfect weather the whole way up pretty much."

It would have been a long trip driving halfway up the

South Island to then get a three-hour ferry ride to Wellington and practically drive the entire length of the North Island. Callum admired his friend's patience with travelling a distance that could have been an hour flight instead.

"Just as well you like it since you gotta drive all the way back," Garrick said.

"Yeah. It isn't too bad. The main hassle was just getting a sore back from being cramped in the car so long." Tim rolled his shoulders back, wincing.

"Is your back still sore?" Garrick asked.

"Yeah. I'm hoping a couple more good sleeps and it'll come right."

"What you need is a good back rub, mate," Garrick said. "That'll take care of it."

"Ha. You reckon?" Tim smirked.

"Yep. I swear by them. I go every Friday to a masseuse here to get rid of work stress." Garrick put his drink down and patted the space of floor between his legs. "Sit down. I can do it now for you."

Tim laughed. "Nar, bro. It's okay."

"Don't be a pussy, Tim. I know what I'm doing." Garrick tapped the floor with his foot, encouraging Tim to take a seat between his legs. "Ask, Callum. I'm good with my hands."

Callum's eyes widened. "Uh-um… yeah, Garrick's really good with his hands."

Tim cast Callum a suspicious look before shrugging. "Fuck it. Why not." He scooted forward off the couch 'till his butt was planted on the floor. He slid over the carpet so he was sat right in front of Garrick, his shoulders at the perfect level for a massage.

Garrick laced his fingers together, cracking his knuckles. He blew on his fingers, warming them up then placed his hands upon Tim's shoulders and began to rub.

Tim's eyes shuddered immediately and he lolled his head back. "Ahhh, that's the shit."

"Yep. This is how you get rid of aches and pains." Garrick grinned over at Callum.

Callum was surprised Tim had agreed to the back rub but his face looked soft and droopy from all the booze and pot which might explain his relaxed state at being touched by another man. Callum watched on as Garrick's strong hands worked their way into Tim's shoulders. The sight made him a little jealous that it wasn't him being treated to such affection. The room fell silent as Garrick continued massaging Tim's back and shoulders.

"Fuck it's awfully quiet," Tim said. He opened his eyes, a groggy smile planted across his lips. "You look bored, man."

"Nar, I'm all good." Callum coughed up a fake smile.

"He's just feeling left out," Garrick said.

"Maybe you can have a turn next," Tim offered. "The G star's bloody good."

You don't have to tell me that.

"Callum can help," Garrick blurted. "Come put yourself to use and rub Tim's feet."

Tim laughed, assuming Garrick was joking. Callum could see the order was no joke.

"Come on," Garrick urged. "Be nice to ya buddy. You ain't seen him in how long? You should be nice to him."

Tim's drunken smile slipped into a giggle again. "I don't think Callum wants to rub my feet."

"Of course he does," Garrick said, casting Callum a stormy glare. "Don't you?"

Rather than respond, Callum put his drink down and crossed the room, sinking to his knees in front of Tim's bent-up legs.

Tim's sleepy eyes widened. "Fucking hell. You actually want to rub my feet for me?"

He could feel Garrick's eyes commanding him. "Yeah, man." Callum said, shrugging. "Why not." Thankfully Tim was too pissed to pick up on his lack of enthusiasm or how weird this scene was fast becoming. Callum tapped Tim's shoes and looked at his stoned mate with a questioning smile. "Do you want a foot rub? I don't mind."

"Knock yourself out." Tim said, closing his eyes,

releasing a happy groan as Garrick kneaded his knuckles into his pressure points.

Callum lifted Tim's left foot off the ground, untying the laces and tugged the shoe from his foot to reveal a navy-blue sock. He did the same with Tim's right foot only to discover he was wearing a white sock.

"Odd socks aye," Garrick said in a hushed tone.

Tim nodded. "Yeah, I didn't expect to be outed as an odd sock wearer tonight." He opened his eyes. "But they're clean. I promise." He closed his eyes again, giving in to the massaging pleasure coming from behind.

Callum bit down on his lip and peeled the odd socks away. He stared at Tim's large feet, inspecting them. He wasn't a huge fan of feet. They were meant for walking on, not to be touched as far as Callum was concerned. Still, he was surprised to see that the lanky Tim had pleasant looking feet; high arches and perfect toes. He took a deep breath and picked up Tim's left foot and began rubbing, massaging the sole with his thumbs.

Tim let out a happy sigh. "This is the life, boys."

"It sure is," Garrick answered. He stroked the side of Tim's neck with his fingertips. "Those look like some big ass feet you got there, Tim."

"Yeah, man. Size 13." Tim chuckled, wiggling his toes. "I love walking bare foot at the beach. All the chicks see how big they are and think I have a huge cock."

Callum rolled his eyes. Tim was so drunk that he had no filter to stop any bullshit coming out of his mouth.

"But do you have the goods to back it up," Garrick said.

"I ain't had any complaints." Tim's face was so relaxed now, he looked like he could melt.

"True." Garrick flicked his eyes down to Callum's feet. "I guess if shoe size and cock size are related then Callum would be the smallest."

The observation made the drunken Tim laugh while Callum tried to keep himself from telling Garrick to go fuck himself. He knew this was another cheap dig designed to remind Callum of who the *bigger* man was between them. "Don't we wear the same size?" Callum said, hoping to level the field.

"Nar. I wear 11's. You're just a 9," Garrick replied speedily.

He was right. Callum found it weirdly flattering that Garrick knew such a random detail about him. But then Garrick knew more than just that body measurement.

Garrick suddenly pulled his hands away. "Take your top off, Tim. It'll make it easier to get this knot out of your back."

"I have a knot?" Tim frowned.

"Yeah, man. Right…. Heeeere." Garrick pressed a finger to a hidden spot, making Tim squirm.

Without questioning, Tim opened his eyes again and lowered his hands, peeling his shirt up off of his body. He threw it to the side and leant back, waiting for Garrick to continue.

Callum let his eyes drift up Tim's body, sizing-up his lean torso. His chest was smooth aside from stray hairs around his pink nipples. His skin had a very faint tan, nothing as golden as Callum's but definitely darker than the paler Garrick. A trail of brown hair began at his navel, travelling in a wide line feeding down below the waistline of his jeans. His stomach no longer had abs like Callum had suspected. Tim was far from fat but his tummy appeared soft, not rock hard like Garrick's. It was strange to be looking at Tim in this way but Callum couldn't help it. Garrick had opened his eyes to male beauty and he found himself looking at Tim in a way he had never done before. A small part of Callum suspected Garrick wanted him to do this; check Tim out. He also worried if this was Garrick's way of trying to push limits that shouldn't be pushed.

It's okay. Even if Garrick is stupid enough to suggest anything, Tim won't let it happen. The thought was reassuring. Callum knew that he wanted to spend the night with Garrick in his bed but to get that he had to do as he was told. Hence, cradling Tim' large foot in his hands. So, provided he did what Garrick asked, he was fine, he would earn his fuck. Callum was relying on Tim to shut anything dubious down. And Tim would. He loved pussy. He didn't do dudes. He wasn't gay, bi or anything like that.

Not like me...

The conversation had died again and the three of them sat there in this bizarre massage circle like a game of twister. Garrick worked his hands deeply into Tim's back while Callum alternated between rubbing each of Tim's long skinny feet. With Tim having his eyes closed, Callum used this opportunity to sneak little looks up at Garrick who would return sexy smiles in-between concentrating on Tim's pleasure.

"You have nice tits for a dude," Garrick said playfully, looking down at Tim's chest.

"Aww shucks," Tim half-laughed.

"Do you work out? You seem quite defined." Garrick placed his hands to Tim's head, working his fingers into Tim's scalp with deft-like movements.

"Not at all," Tim answered, unaware that Garrick wasn't meaning what he said. "This is all natural. Probably helps I'm so tall." He slapped a palm to his chest.

Garrick dropped his hands down to push Tim's hand out of the way, he began rubbing over the complimented area. Stroking up and down over Tim's chest, tweaking his nipples.

Tim's eyes remained close, his mouth slightly ajar. He seemed too lost to the tender touches to pick up anything sexual attached to Garrick's sensual stroking.

Jealousy burned Callum like a naked flame from seeing Garrick touch Tim this way.

It's me you should be touching like that. Not him!

Garrick continued to run his blunt nails up and down Tim's torso, going as low as his tummy, his fingertips touching the edges of Tim's jeans, then clawing his way back up slowly. He pressed his knees into Tim's sides, squeezing. "Feel good?" Garrick whispered, resting his chin on Tim's bare shoulder.

Tim nodded, his eyes half-lidded.

"All you need now is some hot chick to give you a blowie," Garrick added.

Tim's chest rose with a laugh. "Now that would be the perfect touch."

"I know right." Garrick said, his mouth dipping close to Tim's ear. "Some nice wet lips wrapped around your cock, juicing you up. Best way to finish off a massage."

Tim groped his crotch, groaning affirmatively. "Fuck man, don't put ideas in my head. I'll end up with blue balls."

"We can't have that." Garrick chuckled, pulling his head away. "Good thing I know someone 'round here good at sucking dick."

Tim shifted in his sitting spot, turning his face to look up at Garrick. "What's her name?" Intrigue lacing his voice.

Garrick smiled wickedly. "Callum."

CHAPTER TWENTY

Callum arranged his face to a shocked expression. He felt like he should have been surprised by the statement, but he wasn't. This was the risk Garrick had talked about; Callum could feel it in his bones. This was no fucking joke. He stopped rubbing Tim's foot, just gripping it tightly in his hand, waiting for his straight pal's reaction.

Tim's eyes opened, staring ahead at Callum. He frowned momentarily then burst out with a deep belly laugh. "Fucking classic. I know you're both trying to freak me out."

Callum shot a coy smile back, relieved to see Tim not believe the ridiculous comment.

"I'm serious," Garrick said flatly. "You can see how well I have trained him. He's rubbing your feet for you so if I tell him to suck your cock, then yep… he *will* suck your cock."

Tim's laughter rested. He squinted, his bloodshot eyes trying to grapple the sight of Callum in front of him holding his foot.

Callum had an outward calmness to his exterior but on the inside he was shaking with nerves. How Tim chose to interpret the situation could have some major consequences. Then he saw it. A slight twinge in the drunken Tim's face like he was letting his guard down.

"Is he telling the truth?" Tim asked, staring at Callum. "You would suck my cock?" His face was a mixture of shock and disgust.

Callum flicked his eyes at Garrick who stared back with a look that said *your lips belong to me*. He gulped. "Umm…" Callum's words escaped him. He couldn't bring himself to shatter the heterosexual image Tim had of him. Once that broke, all the years of friendship between them would feel tainted. But at the same time he was driven by a strong need to please Garrick. He was torn.

"Just give the word and Callum will give you the blowjob of your life," Garrick said. "I can personally vouch for him that he is a great little cock sucker."

"If you are actually being serious, I'm sorry, but that's a bit too fucking queer for my liking."

"Ain't nothing queer about someone sucking your dick, Tim," Garrick said. "It'll be Callum with a cock in his mouth. Not me or you."

Suddenly, Callum felt like he wasn't even in the room, just an item they were speaking about. He was glad for the alcohol in his system, it helped numb the shame of what he was enduring. It would also probably give him the courage to go to places he never thought he would. *Between Tim's legs.*

An unspoken hierarchy often existed between men. Just like Garrick was unofficially the alpha male over him, Callum had always been the one above Tim. If Garrick made him do this then Callum knew that the invisible authority he held over Tim would be stripped away forever. Pleasing Garrick was one thing but to become viewed less in Tim's eyes was a humiliating and daunting prospect.

"Yep." Garrick went back to rubbing Tim's shoulders. "Just unwind, mate. Let Callum take care of it. It will be the best blowie in your life. Trust me. He will swallow too."

I will? Callum had not even swallowed Garrick yet. Sure, he had licked up leftovers but he hadn't swallowed a whole load. The idea of another man ejaculating seed into his mouth felt dirty. Misty had never even done that for him in all the years they dated and as hot as it would have been to see her do it, he never expected her to. Yet, Garrick didn't seem concerned to offer him the same respect.

"If this is a joke, then you two deserve an academy award cos this is getting all too fucking realistic," Tim said, gifting another lifeline for them to bail on this creepy and awkward gauntlet.

Just fucking drop it, Garrick, Callum pleaded in his mind. *Drop it now and we can pretend it was one big joke.*

Garrick laughed softly in Tim's ear. "This isn't a joke."

Tim frowned, nerves showing through on his drunken face. "It's not?"

"Nope." Garrick returned to stroking his fingertips over Tim's shoulders, pacifying him. "Callum. I want you to be a good *slut* and kiss Tim's foot and ask him nicely for the privilege of sucking his cock."

"Nice one," Tim groaned sarcastically. "Okay, cunts. I'm calling your bluff." Tim wiggled his toes. "Come on, Callum, kiss my foot and ask me then." He chuckled, eager to expose what he no doubt assumed to be a joke.

Callum hesitated. He went to drop Tim's foot and abandon the mission but the thought of his lonely, empty bed urged him to earn Garrick's company. He chewed on his lip, knowing that whatever he did next would damage at least one friendship. If he relented, and did as he was told, then Tim and him would never be the same. But if he disobeyed this order then Garrick would probably refuse to explore the sexual path they had been on.

The dilemma was horrible. Both men looked at him, waiting to see what he would do. Garrick's steely face, urging him on, Tim's cheeky grin waiting to slip out a laugh as the *joke* was uncovered. Callum gave into his maleness and let his little brain make the decision for him. He gently raised Tim's foot closer to his face and kissed the smooth sole of his foot. "Tim, can I have the privilege of sucking your cock?"

Garrick's eyes lit up, pleased to see the order obeyed.

Tim sat there shocked. A cool realisation that this was real coming over his posture.

Callum kissed his foot again. "Please," he whispered.

"Fucking hell," Tim exhaled loudly. He ran a hand through his hair. "You are actually offering to suck my cock?"

Callum nodded, half-expecting to be kicked away.

Tim stared at the floor, biting his bottom lip like he was thinking over what to do. Finally, he looked Callum in the face and arched his eyebrows, drumming his fingers over his jean-clad crotch.

He's fucking saying yes!

Callum lowered Tim's foot to the floor and shuffled forward between Tim's open legs. He flicked Tim a quick look to see if it was okay to proceed.

Tim gave him a slight nod.

Callum reached out, fiddling with Tim's belt. His shaky fingers struggled with the belt buckle. Once it was unlocked, Callum fiddled with the button on his friend's jeans, pulling down the cold metal zip, loosening the pants.

Callum grabbed the sides of Tim's jeans and began to pull. Tim raised his ass off the floor so Callum could drag them down. As the jeans snaked down, Callum got to see just how long and toned Tim's legs were. Covered in a down of fine brown hair, Tim did have nice legs for a guy, Callum thought. When the jeans bunched at Tim's ankles, Callum tugged them over his mate's feet, freeing him. He tossed the jeans aside and stared down at Tim's bulge covered in a pair of red briefs. Under that red material was a piece of Tim Chadwick that Callum had never seen. A piece he should never see. But now he was about to more than see it; he was about to taste it.

Tim looked mesmerised by what was happening. His relaxed face muscles gave away just how drunk he was. Callum assumed it was the booze they had to thank for Tim allowing this same-sex suck. Without alcohol, Tim would have run away long before now.

If he were going to wreck their friendship and assign himself to being bottom of the pecking order then Callum would do it properly. He would give Tim Chadwick the blowjob of his life. Callum craned his neck down and placed his tongue just above Tim's ankle, slowly licking his way up over the prickly leg hair covering Tim's calves. Callum let his tongue climb higher, past the knee, crossing the thin tan line halfway up Tim's inner thighs where the skin became smoother. His mouth collided into Tim's squishy balls encased in the underwear. Callum pressed his face into the bulge, feeling the strong heat radiating from Tim's privates. He clawed at the underwear, tearing the briefs halfway down Tim's thighs.

Tim raised his legs up speedily, letting Callum completely remove the red briefs. The speed at which he wanted to be naked told Callum that his mate was damn horny to be sucked.

He really wants me to do this.

Callum looked down and saw what he was about to suck. Below a nest of trimmed brown pubes Tim's meat was flaccid and draped over a hefty sac of shaved balls. Callum hadn't seen too many scrotums in his life, but he was pretty sure Tim owned the biggest balls in town. The fuckers were huge and he imagined they brewed enormous torrents of jizz.

Callum dove in, eager to show Garrick how dutiful he could be. He scooped Tim's soft cock into his mouth and sucked.

Tim shuddered, his entire body jolting as soon as Callum's lips locked around his prick. His feet jerked around as if he were being tickled.

Shame seeped through Callum as he absorbed the salty taste of Tim's cock. He had had the same reaction both times with Garrick—an emasculating embarrassment—and although this was not his first time sucking a cock, the sensation still held a taboo aura of the unknown.

This feels like I'm breaking something… this is wrong.

Whatever innocence they had shared was obliterated inside his mouth as he sucked the penis of his boyhood friend. What he had done with Garrick seemed different, they had only known each other as adults. Tim though, wasn't the same. Callum and Tim had grown up together, been friends since primary school and somehow that made this all the more creepy and awkward.

Tim's cock remained soft as Callum gobbled it with spit, he began to worry this wasn't going to work. Besides the obvious hurdle of Tim being straight, Callum suspected this would be a hard-fought battle against brewer's droop.

Just suck. Suck hard. Suck him good. Garrick's relying on you.

He placed his hands upon Tim's thighs, rubbing his palms up and down before going higher and playing with his mate's big balls. Callum forced himself to commit to the dick-sucking chore. He continued sucking his friend's flaccid tool, tracing his fingers along Tim's low-hanging scrotum.

Then...

a pulsing spasm.

and another...

Tim's cock began to swell in Callum's mouth, growing steadily with every little twitch. It turned out he wasn't too drunk to get it up. This was a man who was horny and was reacting positively to the warmth of a wet mouth.

"Fuuuuck," Tim sighed loudly. He dropped his hands to the back of Callum's head, twirling his fingers in his hair, pushing him down to keep deep-throating his dick.

Callum slobbered his mate's shaft, feeling a strange sense of pride at managing to get a straight bloke hard. He could feel how hot and erect Tim was now. He pulled his face back, letting himself see the full extent of what Tim had to offer.

What the...?

Callum was surprised to see that his tall mate did not have a huge cock to match his huge balls and large feet. He was probably five-and-a-half inches long and his shaft was more slender than it was thick. It almost looked pretty, if a cock cold be called such a thing. Aside from surprise, Callum felt a relief to find out he didn't have the smallest cock in the room. Still, it didn't change the fact that he was lower down the sex ladder in this exchange. He was the one doing the pleasing—not Tim.

Garrick noticed that Callum had stopped sucking. "Lick his balls clean. Show your mate just how much you've missed him."

The harsh tone jabbed Callum's already-dented pride. He broke his gaze away from admiring the slim prick and dropped his face low to the ground and begun to tongue at Tim's huge sac. Pressing his nose into Tim's scrotum, Callum was fascinated at how soft and smooth the loose skin felt against his face. Tim's balls rolled over his tongue, their weight heavy and full; this was a man who needed to cum. As he licked and slurped from one nut to the next, Callum could smell a faint whiff of ball sweat.

This was fucking humiliating; he was literally licking Tim Chadwick's balls clean. And even though he was ashamed beyond belief to be on the floor scooping his mouth under his best mate's shaved sac of scrotum, Callum could feel in his pants a boner coming on.

I'm getting off on this!

It had been a fucking weird thing the past week to accept that he was attracted to Garrick, but he was now discovering that he was also attracted to being subservient. He may have been being treated like he was down low but he still felt dizzy like he had vertigo. The submissive realisation filled his mind almost as much as Tim's big balls smothered his face.

"Fuck yeah," Tim groaned, pressing the back of Callum's head.

"I told you the slut was good, didn't I?" Garrick said casually.

Slut. It was a derogatory term, but he said it so pleasantly it almost felt like Callum had been called by his first name.

Tim grabbed Callum's hair, yanking his face up to look him in the eyes. "Oh man... shit... you suck dick like a champ." he said between halting breaths. A cruel smirk began to spread across his lips. "Who'd of thought I'd be getting noshed off by Tasman Heights High's star soccer player." He gave a husky wheeze of laughter and shoved Callum's face back down to his smooth nuts.

It appeared Tim was amused by the position he was in, lording the power Garrick was generously sharing with him. It was no surprise. Callum too would enjoy such a thorough servicing.

The darker side of male pride meant that this was a thrill, a way for one bloke to stamp authority over another. As much as Tim loved his cock being sucked, Callum doubted how much of the thrill was sexual as it was mental. For Tim, this was a one up on a friend who had always been more popular, always received more female attention. The more sucking and licking, the more Tim probably felt like he was getting some sort of karmic vengeance on the once king-of-the-school Callum.

A part of Callum wanted to spit Tim's balls out and tell him to get fucked, remind Tim that he was the one lower down. But Callum couldn't. He couldn't ever claim to be the bigger man. Not now he had sucked the guy's dick and given his balls a thorough tongue bath.

"Take your clothes off, slut," Garrick barked.

Callum spat Tim's nuts out and shot up, his orders had been given. He kicked his shoes off and stripped out of all of his clothes 'till he was every bit as naked as Tim.

"Fucking hell," Tim chuckled. "You've got a fucking boner. What a fag."

So do you, dickhead.

"Yep. Callum here really gets off on cock. That's why he's so good at it." Garrick rest back into the couch, smiling.

Tim looked Callum up and down, checking him out. His eyes zoned in on his penis, comparing sizes no doubt.

That's right. It's bigger than yours. Callum wished Tim could read his mind and hear the mental sass he was giving.

"How would you like to suck my cock for a bit, slut?" Garrick grinned, rubbing his crotch.

Callum nodded. "Yes please, sir."

"He called you sir!" Tim sniggered. "This is fucking classic."

"Of course he does," Garrick said.

Callum got back down on his knees, shuffling closer to Garrick. Tim slid to the side, giving him room, watching in glee to see Callum suck another cock.

Garrick wasted no time in unzipping and flopping his dick out. "It's all yours, slut."

Callum didn't fuck about. He leaned in, dropping his mouth over Garrick's semi-erect member, sucking it with impatient force. *Fuck yes!* He loved this cock. This was what it was all about. He adored this man and what he had between his legs. He would suck Tim because he had to, but he would suck Garrick because he wanted to. The difference was

177

noticeable to all in the room, Callum's moaning and hungry hands clawing under Garrick's shirt left no illusion as to whose cock he preferred.

"Fucking hell," Tim blurted. "He's chowing down on your meat."

"Yeah. He prefers them big," Garrick answered briskly.

Callum had to force himself not to smile at the sly dig.

"Apparently so," Tim mumbled, not disputing the fact.

While Tim had not leaked a single drop of precum, it didn't take long for Garrick to be oozing like a leaky tap in Callum's mouth, feeding him the delicious seed he craved. Even though he had only sucked Garrick off twice before, there was a familiarity to his cock that felt comforting. Callum knew this tool, he knew to slurp and suck and how best to manoeuvre his mouth over the curve. He drove his tongue into Garrick's piss slit, digging for more of the stud's tasty cum.

Garrick began to rub his neck tenderly. "Good work, slut. Good work."

"Thank you, sir," Callum spluttered back.

Tim laughed again, entertained by Callum's slavish attitude.

Callum ignored Tim's nasty laughter, trying to focus only on Garrick's precum soaked rod. The room fell quiet, the only noise coming from the sloppy sucks of Callum's lips. He could feel Tim and Garrick's eyes burning in on him, watching as he fed himself inch after inch of hard dick. Callum's eyelids became drowsy and his jaw began to slack from the vigorous workout his mouth was doing. Just when he wasn't sure he could give anymore, Garrick tapped his shoulder and told him to stop.

"You've earnt a break," Garrick said. He smiled down at him affectionately before glancing towards Tim who sat on the floor beside Callum. "Would you like to try?"

Tim frowned, shaking his head. "Nar, bro. I don't think I could do that," he said in a slurred speech. The smell of alcohol on his breath was thick.

"It's easy as," Garrick replied. "You saw Callum do it."

"Yeah, but he's a fag... I'm not."

The word stung like a bee. Sure, Tim was using it as a throwaway reference but it really packed a punch for Callum now. He knew he would never utter the word again himself.

Garrick reached out and kindly stroked Tim's jaw. "That's a shame. I'd love to see you try. Be quite an honour to be sucked off by someone so good-looking."

A primal jealousy gripped Callum. Compliments were not to be shared around.

Tim chuckled. "I'm not that good-looking, bro."

"You really are," Garrick said, his voice sensually disarming. "Besides, you only live once, right?" He gripped his cock in his hand, squeezing it, showing off its mighty size.

Callum watched as Tim's face went from one of revulsion at the idea to one of questioning.

Garrick swivelled his index finger around the tip of his cock, scooping some of his precum up with his fingertip. He extended it out towards Tim, smiling encouragingly. He didn't wait for Tim to respond and dabbed his finger gently against Tim's bottom lip. "Open up," he whispered.

Tim defied all odds and opened his mouth, slowly sucking down on Garrick's cum-covered finger. He sucked for five seconds then slurped his lips free and swallowed. He smiled nervously at what he had just done.

"See. That wasn't so bad, was it?" Garrick said.

"I guess not." Tim sighed almost silently.

"Come on," Garrick said softly like he was taming a feral animal. His eyes were glossed with trustworthiness, similar to the way he had looked at Callum the first night they fooled around together.

Tim's body was loose. The alcohol had loosened him up enough to go this far, his drunk mind giving in to the invite. He teetered closer and began to blush, giggling. "I can't believe I'm about to try this."

Garrick rubbed the nape of Tim's neck, softly pushing

his face lower.

Tim took a deep breath and kissed the sticky tip of Garrick's cock, licking his lips. Tim shot Callum a quick glance—pleading with him not to watch. Callum ignored the visual request, taking great delight in watching Tim hover his open mouth over Garrick's manhood and begin to suck.

Callum was in awe at what he was seeing. It was one thing to trick a drunken Tim into getting naked and receiving a blowjob…but to get him to give one… that was the stuff of legend. But if anyone could pull a stunt like this off then it would be Garrick Masters.

Garrick sat there like a king, enjoying the feel of inexperienced lips wrapped around his thick cock. He stroked his fingers through Tim's mop of brown hair, giving Callum a sly wink like this was all for his benefit.

Tim's eyes were rammed shut. He was only managing to suck the top two inches, like he was still getting used to the feeling of having another man's dick in his mouth. Callum knew what that was like.

"Help him out, slut," Garrick said, pointing at his lap.

Callum moved forward, positioning himself next to Tim so that their naked bodies were touching. He licked near the base of Garrick's cock, stray pubes tickling his tongue while Tim continued to slobber the top two inches of Garrick's fuckmeat. Their faces rubbed together, stubble scratching one another.

Callum didn't know why, but he felt compelled to touch his fellow cocksucker. He dropped a hand down and seized hold of Tim's penis, playing with it between his fingers. To his surprise, Tim returned the favour, reaching down and groping Callum's balls, jiggling them in his hand.

"It's good to see my sluts playing nice together," Garrick boasted in piss-taking fashion. Just like that, Tim had been thrown into the *slut* category.

Some of Callum's ill will towards Tim disappeared. His drunk mate may have mocked Callum's subservient role but now he too was a servant. He may not have been as low down as Callum, but he still had a dick in his mouth.

"Kiss for me. I want to see you sluts kiss," Garrick said, testing the waters of his control.

Callum slurped up Garrick's shaft 'till he met with Tim's lips waiting for him atop of Garrick's prick. Their tongues touched, sliding around the gooey tip of Garrick's penis, before ramming them in each other's mouths, sharing the taste of sweet, sweet semen.

Tim pulled away, wiping his mouth.

Callum thought that was it, but then Tim leaned back in, pressing their lips together with more force and determination, he took control of Callum's mouth, licking and sucking. The kiss was messy and ravishing. Tim's tongue darted around like a fish in a barrel, pointless and desperate.

Callum squeezed Tim's cock tightly, receiving a soggy gasp. In return, Tim tugged on Callum's smooth nuts making him moan wildly. They kept hold of each other's privates as they continued to kiss only inches above Garrick's cock. By now Tim's spastic tongue thrusts had slowed down and their tongues were wrapped together in a sensual harmony, swapping spit in an agreed rhythm.

You're not too bad at kissing.

It was weird to be learning this about his boyhood friend, but then he had already learned so much. Discovering Tim was a good kisser didn't make a huge difference. He wasn't as good as Garrick but then no one was.

Callum began to wank Tim's cock, wanting to get his mate off and feel his dick shoot a load. The fast jerk was working and Tim's breaths passing into Callum's mouth became ragged and wet. Just as Callum thought he had fired the fleshy gun in his hands, Garrick ripped their kiss apart, pulling at both their hair.

"Stop! No one is losing their lollies until I say so," he growled. He narrowed his eyes and let his voice dance across their faces like a mystery, "I think it's time to really get this game night started."

Callum gulped. Things already felt like they had begun. Oh, how wrong he was.

The games were only about to begin…

CHAPTER TWENTY-ONE

Callum clamped his lips shut and breathed through his nose, waiting to see which direction Garrick was trying to send the evening. It was already steamy in this room. Fuck, Callum had already sucked Tim's cock and now they had been kissing, hovering just inches above Garrick's dick as they swapped spit and moans. It didn't seem like things needed a boost. But then Garrick Masters didn't do anything by halves.

Tim had his trademark goofy smile aimed at Callum. "Fuck, bro, this is fucking trippy."

Callum suspected that come the morning Tim would have a hangover as heavy as his impending regret.

"It's a good thing you didn't cum, 'cos I'm the one who decides when you both blow," Garrick said gruffly, like he was the owner of orgasms.

Callum blinked—stunned—while Tim chuckled, seemingly unaware of how intense the situation was.

"You need more practise, Tim. Wrap your lips 'round me again." Garrick then focused his attention to Callum. "And you." He pointed. "Lick his ass out."

"What?" Callum balked.

"You heard me," Garrick said. "Lick his ass out."

"Nar, bro. I don't want him stickin nuffin in there," Tim said, struggling to string the sentence together.

Garrick looked calm but authoritative. "You'll love it. I promise. He's already sucked your cock, be a shame not to let him lick you out." He ruffled Tim's hair affectionately.

"I'm not a fag though," Tim quipped.

That fucking word again!

"I know, mate. That would be Callum," Garrick said.

Tim snickered, flicking Callum a shit-eating grin.

You just sucked his cock too, Tim. I don't think you're exactly 100% straight at the moment.

"Just chill out, enjoy my cock, and let the slut lick you out nice n good." Garrick patted Tim's head, sending a disarming smile.

Callum felt left out. No niceties for him, just degrading orders. He watched on as Garrick worked his magic fingers through Tim's hair, making the tall guy appear drowsy. Tim's face gave way to a droopy smile. What the fuck was it about Garrick that made him so amazing and able to reduce people to melting messes and do as he pleased. It was almost witchy how he cast spells. He had a gift to evoke passion and Callum found himself wishing Tim wasn't here. Wishing Garrick's fingers were reserved for him, and him only.

Garrick lured Tim's head back down towards his crotch. "Come on, buddy, sort me out."

"Okay," Tim mumbled. He licked the tip of Garrick's stiff prick, swirling his tongue around the leaky slit. Garrick pushed the back of Tim's head, sliding his dick further inside Tim's mouth and stretching his lips. Rather than struggle, Tim accepted the engorged pipe he was being fed. He slurped and sucked the sexual instrument like he was blowing a harmonica.

Callum watched on in awe as a sadistic chill tickled his spine. He wondered if Tim would have been quite so keen to suck on something that had—twice now—been buried balls-deep inside Callum's churning shitter.

Garrick continued to rub his hand through Tim's hair, congratulating him. Despite having his cock out, Garrick was still fully clothed, adding another level of dominance to him that Tim and Callum lacked through being fully naked. His eyes locked on Callum and he mouthed, *Lick him out!*

Callum gulped. He shuffled backwards so he was sitting directly behind Tim's hunched over form. Tim had his head buried in Garrick's lap, sucking the cock that Callum wanted so badly. Instead, he was dealing with the tail end of the situation—Tim's ass. He absorbed the sight of Tim's long physique that from this angle had a lithe quality. His buttocks were unblemished pale mounds that appeared smooth aside from the strip of stray hairs lining his crack.

Callum's gut somersaulted, knowing he was about to stick his tongue inside the hairy trail. Out of nowhere, his mind hurled him down memory lane to younger days, walking to school with Tim. He wondered what his teenaged self would say if he was told that one day he would have his tongue inside his tall mate's ass and suck his cock.

Probably, "Fuck off!"

Callum's breath gusted out, accepting he was about to do another thing he never thought he would do in his life. He prudently placed his hands on each cheek, opening Tim's ass up like the pages of a book. Tim's dim hole looked clean and tight. Callum could tell just by looking at the tiny muscle that this was an ass that had never been invaded, not like his own cavity which had been opened twice by Garrick.

He lowered his face to the haired line of Tim's crack, dabbing his tongue along the entrance, taste testing what he was about to eat out. Tim's ass had a hot scent, a faint bitterness clinging in the depths of his crease. Callum licked swiftly up and down, wetting his mate's ass hairs. Tim groaned in response, his backside shaking. Callum repeated the action; up and down, then doing circles, exploring the taste of something previously untouched. It wasn't like he enjoyed the moist flavour but he did enjoy the reaction he was causing.

Tim writhed and squirmed. He broke free from sucking Garrick's cock. "Whoa," he murmured, warped with pleasure from what Callum was doing to him.

"Just keep sucking," Garrick said, shoving Tim's face back down.

Callum didn't let up, he swivelled his tongue directly over Tim's hole, dabbing it with slick licks, getting more pleasing moans from his tall friend who was back to sucking dick. After a while the taste of hot ass got lost in saliva and Callum found himself wishing he could do more than just lick. He spread Tim's cheeks as far as they would go, nuzzling his face into his mate's whiskery crack, pushing his tongue right down on the untaken hole, wanting to slip inside. He wanted to open Tim up; open his ass and mind to a new realm of pleasure, but Tim's hole fought back, clenching like it was trying to banish Callum's probing tongue.

Callum dropped his hand down, smoothing his palm over Tim's leg, pressing down, his fingers curling over his tender inner thigh. He wanted to fuck Tim so badly. He wanted to fuck both men so badly, but he knew that if any fucking happened tonight, it was his ass on the chopping block.

Garrick looked down at him, their gazes locking over Tim's butt cheeks. His hips bucked gently, fucking Tim's mouth as he pouted his lips like he was blowing Callum a kiss. The flirting was torturous. It made Callum want to try even harder to impress his asshole's virginity taker.

Callum pulled his mouth away from Tim's ass and flopped onto his back, sliding himself under Tim's spread legs like a mechanic rolling on a creeper to inspect a vehicle.

Tim's balls dangled above his face like church bells. Callum tugged at them, making his friend sit down so he could continue feeding on his hot ass. Tim obliged, plopping down heavily and smothering Callum's face with his shaved sac and sweet cheeks. Callum manoeuvred his mouth 'till he found Tim's crack, slipping his tongue inside and continued to thrust his tongue along the soggy ass hairs and licked-out hole. As he pressed his tongue in deep, he gripped hold of Tim's firm calf muscles, raking his fingers up and down.

Tim pressed his ass down harder, wanting more tongue action. The heat from being smothered made Callum' face break out in a sweat. This was so fucking erotic. Callum's cock was rock-hard and his balls aching they were so full. Tim was the same, his stiff cock slapping Callum's forehead the more he bounced and writhed.

The room had become an orchestra of sex; slurps from ass licking and cock sucking, mingled moans from all three men.

Callum let go of Tim's legs and wriggled his arms up

closer to the couch, trying to find Garrick's feet. He needed to touch him, he need to feel close to this man who felt like his owner. With Tim's balls covering his eyes, Callum's hand fished around aimlessly trying to find a piece of Garrick to hold on to. Finally, he felt Garrick's socked foot. He slipped his fingers up inside the leg hole of Garrick's pants and began rubbing the hairs on his leg. It was such a small patch of body, but it felt like a piece of heaven beneath his fingers.

Just as Callum began to creep his fingers higher, Garrick shook his foot, ridding himself of the desperate grasp. Callum's heart sank at being so rudely shaken off.

Suddenly, Tim rose, removing his ass and suffocating balls.

What's going on?

Callum looked down the length of his naked body towards his feet and could see Garrick standing there. He slid out from under Tim to see what was happening.

"Sit over there, slut," Garrick said, clicking his fingers and pointing.

Callum crawled out from between Tim's legs and sat to the side where Garrick had pointed.

"Watch and learn," Garrick said with a smirk.

Callum frowned, unsure what he was referring to.

Tim looked dozy and flushed, still curved over the couch. "Fuck, bro. This is one helluva game night." He chuckled, slurping back some of the spit seeping from the corner of his freshly-fucked mouth.

Garrick raised each of his legs, one at a time, peeling his socks off before planting his bare feet to the floor and begin to unbutton his pants.

Finally! He's getting naked too.

Callum watched Garrick shimmy out of his pants, freeing his thick, strong legs. Next to come off was his shirt, exposing the hairy chest that Callum had come to love.

Even completely naked Garrick oozed undeniable control. His unwavering dominance was no doubt aided from being the proud owner of the biggest cock in the room.

Callum sat, stuck in a trance, wondering what sort of

perverse move was to follow.

Garrick dropped to his knees, sucking up saliva and spitting into the palm of his hand.

Slurp. Plip. Slurp. Plip.

He put his hand out and rubbed his fingers into Tim's ass.

"Wh-what are you doing?" Tim asked, his voice timid. "You're not—"

"Shhh," Garrick interrupted, draping himself over Tim's back. "I'm giving you what you want." His hand kept playing at Tim's rear, lubing him up.

"Nar, bro. I really don't want that," Tim replied.

Garrick licked the rim of Tim's ear, biting gently on his earlobe. Little tricks designed to make the tall guest surrender and give himself away. His hand dipped under, grabbing hold of Tim's cock, jacking him slowly. "You want what I want. Don't you?"

Tim went rigid. "What is it you want?".

"To make love to you," Garrick returned. "I've never fucked anyone as hot as you."

How about me? Callum kept his bitterness to himself. It was fucking plain to see that Garrick was using false flattery to get what he wanted. He began to suspect that maybe he too had been the victim of false flattery the night he gave his ass away. Yet, it didn't stop him wanting Garrick. The damage had been done. Callum was hooked.

"Say what?" Tim blushed.

"I've never fucked anyone as hot as you. Guy or girl." Garrick patted Tim's rump. "You're such a handsome fucker. It would be an honour if you let me."

Tim was so stoned and pissed, he appeared to believe the bullshit. He stared Callum directly in the eyes like he was asking what he should do.

Callum arched his eyebrows, encouraging Tim to give in.

Do it! Become like me.

Callum wanted Tim to know what it felt like; being churned and skewered by an ass-splitting cock. Have him share some of the shame. He wanted Tim to be added to Garrick's list of conquests. Maybe then Callum would be less hung up about having had a man's cock in his ass. Someone could share in his secret and be tainted in the same way.

Tim exhaled loudly, rubbing his face. "If I let you do this, it would stay between us, right?"

"Of course, man." Garrick answered quickly. "What happens at game night stays at game night."

"Hmph." Tim chewed on his lip. He still didn't look completely sold on the idea.

Garrick dipped his mouth to Tim's ear and whispered, "Come on, bro, your ass looks so much nicer than this slut's."

He doesn't mean that. He doesn't mean it.

Tim laughed. "If you say so."

"Let me just rubber up," Garrick said, pulling his mouth away from Tim's ear.

Tim's eyes were wide, but he remained bent over serving his ass up. It appeared that Garrick's trick of stirring up friendly rivalry might just work.

CHAPTER TWENTY-TWO

Garrick fished through the pockets of his pants, retrieving a foil-wrapped condom that gleamed in his hand like a weapon. Never before had something designed for safety looked so dangerous. He didn't piss about ripping into the packet and slathering the rubber down his piece. Next, he tore open a sachet of lube, using its glunky contents to wet his shielded shaft. He looked around, trying to find something to wipe his hands on. He plucked up Tim's red briefs, using them like a rag to dry his hands.

"You ready, Tim?" Garrick asked, patting Tim's upturned ass.

Tim hesitated for a moment before nodding gently. "Yep," he whispered.

Garrick eyed Tim's ass with predatory yearning, resembling a lion eyeing its prey. His dark eyes were beastly, a look that evoked as much fear as it did desire. He grazed two fingers down Tim's slick trench, emphasising his internal intent.

"Shit," Tim muttered.

Garrick placed his hand on Tim's hip, the other holding his meat, steering it towards a reluctant virgin hole. A smile licked his lips as he teasingly rubbed the head of his cock against Tim's pucker.

Tim's whole body shook with nerves, his face resembling Callum's a week earlier when he too had encountered the fear of first-times.

Garrick sighed very quietly as he snaked a palm up Tim's spine, caressing him. His hips tapped forward. A firm nudge. His cock claiming another trophy.

Tim's eyes bulged as his mouth creaked a muted moan. The look on his face was one of pained shock—his hole had been breached. He moaned again, louder, as Garrick gave a dense push, feeding him more cock. "Fuck," Tim hissed through clenched teeth, knotting his hands into fists. His entire body appeared to ripple, wracked by full body quakes measuring eight inches on the rectumscale.

"Just relax," Garrick said, rubbing Tim's back. "Let me in…. nice and slow."

Tim grimaced, mashing his lips together as he tried letting the master in.

Callum smiled at his grimacing friend, partly to try and calm him down, but also because he was enjoying seeing Tim in the process of being added to Garrick's list of conquests. He had no idea where these dubious thoughts came from, and although he had an inherent sense they were wrong, he embraced them.

Tim's body writhed while Garrick's surged ahead with a firm slowness that was constantly drilling and feeding Tim's hole inch after inch.

"Good boy, nearly there," Garrick murmured, watching his cock delve deeper.

Tim sucked in a deep breath, trying to loosen up.

Callum found it entertaining to hear Tim—a man who was six-feet-three-inches tall—referred to as *boy*.

Garrick began mixing his slow, steady entry with gentle pumps against Tim's expanding hole. His smile grew wider the deeper his cock dug in, his manhood soon became completely buried inside Tim's butthole. He draped his hairy chest over Tim's back, his crotch grinding skin to skin against Tim's ass.

Callum watched on, switching between Tim's wild gyrations and Garrick's grinding humps. Their thrashing bodies a marvellous spectacle.

"How's it feel to have another man's cock rammed inside you," Garrick taunted, pumping his dick with a sloppy thump inside Tim's ass.

Tim nodded. "It's—okay" he said through gritted teeth.

Garrick reached under, gripping hold of Tim's cock,

giving him a good squeeze. "You like being my bitch then, Tiny Tim?"

Callum nearly snorted at the audacity of the comment. There was no denying what Garrick was calling *tiny*.

"I'm not tiny," Tim replied snottily.

Garrick laughed. He squeezed Tim's cock again. "Yeah, you are. But it's a hot little prick."

Tim went to reply but his words gave way to mumbled moans as Garrick suddenly increased the tempo of his thrusts and began ploughing his ass with ferocious fuck-motions, showing Tim's virgin hole no mercy. He had never gone that hard on Callum. Not even close. The way he fucked was like he was angry, unleashing a tonne of fury designed to wreck Tim's already-battered hole.

Instead of scrambling away, Tim rose to the challenge, embracing his submissive role. He reached behind, clutching Garrick's thudding hips. "Fuck me then, cunt," he gasped.

Garrick halted his thrusts, yanking Tim by the hair and whispered angrily in his ear, "It isn't *cunt*. It's sir to you." He gave a particularly nasty pump of his hips to prove his point.

"Unnnh, fuck." Tim winced. He took a sharp breath and said, "Fuck me, sir. Fuck me with that big dick of yours."

Garrick grinned, pleased for the acknowledgement. He peeled his sweating hairy chest from Tim's back, straightened his body and continued to annihilate Tim's sphincter. He started slapping Tim's buttocks. Stinging smack after stinging smack rained down on Tim's ass, sounding like flip-flops thwacking heels.

Callum couldn't take his eyes away. He was in the midst of what felt like a head-on collision, witnessing two men with giant egos battle for supremacy. Yes, Tim was asking for it but the way Garrick fucked like a monster was skirting the edges of right and wrong. Clung together, their toothsome twisting torsos put on a filthy show; a deliciously dubious deed ... and it was, quite fucking frankly, hot-hot-hot.

Tim had surprised him by begging to be taken harder

and paying tribute to Garrick's authority and size. Maybe it was foolish courage or maybe it was the booze—either way Callum was impressed. He didn't know if he should congratulate or pity Tim for the loose and sore asshole he would wake up with in the morning.

Garrick stopped with the spanking and gave Callum a salacious wink, encouraging him to come closer and see what his cock was doing.

Callum scooched over and peered down to watch Tim's ass being punished.

Garrick slowed his frantic pace, letting Callum see just how his dick worked in another man's ass.

Holy fuck!

He was blown away by the sight of Garrick's fleshy spike stabbing deep within Tim's anal cavern. Callum couldn't believe that the pussy-loving Tim had just under eight inches of fuckmeat sheathed inside his butthole.

So this is what it looks like when he fucks my ass.

Callum had already felt how big Garrick's cock was going inside him, but being able to watch it in action...well, that gave a whole new perspective of how large his mate's shaft really was. It was no small feat to be able to take so much cock. He decided both he and Tim deserved a medal.

The smooth finesse of Garrick's meat going in and out was impressive. He would withdraw nearly all the way out, leaving just the engorged head of his dick inside, then slam back in 'till his hairy balls were squished against the smoothness of Tim's ass.

The rim of Tim's anus clenched around Garrick's thick-rubbered prick, swallowing it tightly. Callum found himself wishing he was the one doing the fucking, he licked his lips knowing how good that virgin ass would feel gripped around his cock. Tim's ass cheeks were red as a sunset from Garrick's firm hand spanking him. Just looking at them felt painful.

"Mmph." Tim groaned every time Garrick's cock impaled him balls-deep.

"Your hole is loosening up nice n good, Tiny Tim."

Garrick grinned. He changed his technique, swirling his hips in little circles, loosening Tim up even more.

Callum gingerly stroked Garrick's thigh wanting to feel part of what was happening.

Garrick flicked his hand away. "Piss off," he muttered, not wanting his rhythm broken.

Knowing that Garrick was off limits, Callum decided to touch Tim instead. He gripped his aching hard cock in his hand and began to rub it up and down Tim's shaking calf muscle, dabbing driblets of precum over his pal's leg hairs. It felt slightly rebellious, like he was rubbing salt into Tim's ego wounds, adding to his ordeal

"Hard enough for ya, Tiny Tim," Garrick grunted snidely.

Tim's face was now smooshed into the couch, making muffled sounds. He let go of Garrick's hips and gave the thumbs up.

"I didn't hear you," Garrick said, a darkness tinging his voice. "Am I fucking you hard enough?"

"Yes..." a quick breath. "Sir." The smallness of Tim's voice was undeniable—he had fully submitted.

Hearing Tim's pitiful response made Garrick focus even more on stuffing his manhood up Tim's clasping rectum. His vocal grunting became laboured, perspiration wetting his forehead and tussled hair. His biceps curled with definition the way he grasped hold of Tim, fucking with masculine confidence, chipping away at Tim's anal virginity like it were the enemy. "Nearly there, Tiny Tim. Nearly. Fucking. There."

Tim groaned loudly; a mix of annoyance at his assigned nick name and a vague effort at encouraging Garrick to finish his fuck.

Callum scooted backwards, not wanting to miss the look on Garrick's face the moment he came. They had been fucking for a good ten minutes but a part of him wanted Tim's ass to keep taking it.

"I'm close... here... it... comes..." Garrick's voice jerked as much as his body did. He slipped his cock out and ripped the rubber off and immediately shoved his swollen prick right back inside Tim's hole.

Whoa….

Callum was spellbound.

He didn't just….

Yes. Yes, he fucking did! Garrick's bare dick was shoved halfway inside Tim's ravished hole, spasming violently as it unloaded hot spunk inside. Garrick's entire body shook and trembled as he kept shooting. He pulled his cock back so that just the tip was stuck in Tim's entrance, making sure he got traces of cum at all sections of his widened passage. Callum watched in horny horror as Garrick's abundant seed began spilling out the edges of Tim's penetrated ass.

Tim remained hunched over, his head planted into the seat of the couch, his breaths hitching. Did he know what was happening?

He soon answered that question.

"Gross, bro. Did you just cum in me?" He shifted forward.

"Wait. I wanna make sure you catch all of it. Callum doesn't need my cum staining his carpet," Garrick said, tapping Tim's rump, not letting him move till he was done. Once his dick had stopped shaking, he pulled out. He locked eyes on Callum. "Suck it clean. That's your job, slut."

Callum hesitated. *But it's just been in Tim…* He didn't have a chance to argue, Garrick stood up and guided his cock straight to Callum's mouth. Begrudgingly Callum opened wide and sucked the head clean, tasting dollops of Garrick's sweet cum. With the layer of slick semen sucked off, he began to taste traces of Tim's ass clinging to Garrick's foreskin. He pulled back, scrunching his face up, not wanting anymore.

Garrick laughed at seeing him grimace, stepped back, and began to fossick through his pants on the floor. He pulled out his cell phone and aimed it at Tim's leaky cum-filled hole.

Click.

"One for the memory book," Garrick said, laughing.

He collected his clothes and stared down at Callum. "Right, I'm gonna go use your shower and clean up." He looked at Tim who appeared frozen in time, stooped over the couch with an orifice that looked like it was leaking milk. "Sort ya mate out. Tiny Tim deserves a good suck to empty his balls after that fine performance." He lowered his hand and slapped Tim on the ass. "You took it so fucking sweet, mate. Good shit." On those belittling words, he wandered off towards the bathroom like he owned the place.

Callum sat on the floor, staring at Tim's behind. He moved in, assessing the aftermath of Garrick's raw deed.

Fuck me...

The length of Tim's crack appeared slick and slippery from the lube, his gaping sphincter white and gooey, filled to the brim with Garrick's swimmers. The rim of his hole looked red and angry. His hole was like a sexual war zone, no longer resembling the tightly-sealed ass Callum had licked out. He pressed his finger to the creamy substance slowly trickling out, the tip of his finger edging inside and swirling in Garrick's hot cum. There was a lot. *A helluva lot.* Tim had been utterly filled.

"Get ya finger out of there," Tim snapped. He lifted his face and turned his body 'round and leant his back against the couch. He sat facing Callum with his knees up and legs open.

Fuck. Please don't leak all on the floor.

Tim's face looked red from being buried against the fabric of the couch for so long. He wheezed out a long slow breath. "Can't say that is how I thought tonight would go," he said, his voice trying to sound light. His dick was more soft than hard, apparently he didn't get off on the feel of being fucked so intrusively.

"Yeah..." Callum faked a smile. "How does it feel?" he pointed between Tim's legs.

"Wet... sticky." Tim laughed without smiling. He seemed way more sober than before. It was as if the booze and pot had been fucked out of him.

"Does it feel like much?"

Tim nodded, frowning.

Callum pitied and envied his friend. Tim didn't appear overly happy to be sat with an ass leaking cum, but at the same time Callum was jealous that Garrick gave Tim something he hadn't yet given him.

Maybe later tonight?

Callum slid between Tim's legs and began to rub the prickly hairs just above his ankle.

Tim gave him a funny look. "What are you doing?"

"He told me to suck your cock."

Tim rolled his eyes. "It's okay, Callum. I don't need you to suck me off. I think shit is weird enough without adding spunking in your gob to the list."

Callum didn't know why but he felt like he had to do this. Garrick had given him the order and even though he wasn't in the room to see, he was obligated. He smiled at Tim. "Then I can't see how swallowing your cum can make things worse."

"You're serious… You'll actually *swallow*?"

Callum nodded.

"What a fag," Tim laughed.

"Says the guy with a load of cum in his ass."

"Touche," Tim mumbled. He sighed and tugged on his cock. "Okay, but don't call me Tiny fucking Tim." He said, trying to sound humorous, but the damage to his usually big ego was undeniable.

"Okay." Callum grabbed hold of his mate's softening cock, playing with it. He gave Tim a sympathetic smile. If shit was going to be weird, he at least wanted Tim to feel better. "And for the record, I think you have a beautiful dick." Callum bowed his head down and placed Tim's meat in his mouth and sucked.

CHAPTER TWENTY-THREE

Callum paced back and forth in the lounge. It had been thirty minutes since Garrick had taken Tim home and he began to suspect that he wasn't coming back. The deal had been that if he did what Garrick wanted then he would get what he wanted—a night together.

He fucking lied.

Callum had done everything. Absolutely everything Garrick had asked of him. He could still taste the final order in his mouth. Swimming in his gut was Tim's semen that he had indeed swallowed.

Despite the weird fucking vibe between them, Tim had still been horny and it didn't take long for him to be gasping and grunting loudly. It turned out that it wasn't only Garrick who was capable of shooting mammoth loads—Tim too brewed piles of spunk. He had moaned erotically as his dick ejaculated sizzling ball juice down Callum's throat. There was so fucking much of it that Callum worried he would spit it over the floor. But he kept his mouth pressed to his mate's cum pipe and made sure he got every drop before swallowing it in one face-grimacing gulp.

Callum stopped pacing and stared up at the clock. "Where the fuck are you, Garrick Masters." He could feel himself getting shitty. Game night had been a fucking surprise from start to finish. He had expected an evening of just the two of them, where he had hoped that maybe they would fool around again. That wishful fantasy had been blown out of the water the moment Garrick appeared at the door with Tim in tow.

It had been great to see Tim again, even if it had dampened Callum's erotic plans at first. It was the first chance they'd had to catch up since Tim moved away, and just as they had started to settle into a comfortable evening, Garrick had gone and done the unthinkable; orchestrating a situation that created the most fucked-up memory you could between lifelong friends.

Is that what he wanted? To make things awkward between us?

It had been uncomfortable throughout the whole ordeal but Callum's horniness and need to impress Garrick had spurred him on, allowing him to neglect the damage that such *fun* was having. It was only after Tim had spoofed in his mouth that the real effect of what they had done became noticeable. Suddenly the room had fallen heavy with mood, an unspoken uneasiness drifting between them as they put their clothes back on and sat in silence, waiting for Garrick to finish in the shower.

Once Garrick did appear he acted like nothing had happened. He didn't even say a word about how he had just manipulated two men into being his sexual minions. Nope, not a word. He just stood there aloof like he always did; cool, calm and confident, running a hand through his wet hair.

Garrick simply jangled his keys and offered Tim a ride home, which Tim had jumped at in a heartbeat. Just like that, they were gone, leaving Callum alone with a used condom laying on the floor. A wrinkled condom that had been slapped over one mate's cock and then deposited into the asshole of another.

They had only been gone a minute before the horny bravado Callum had been clinging to began to crumble. He was so embarrassed that Tim had seen him behaving so subserviently, seeing him at his most pathetic. Tim would never look at him the same again, knowing that Callum had become another man's plaything so willingly.

The only saving grace was how Garrick had well and truly made Tim his servant too, fucking him like a piece of cheap meat. The only difference was—Callum suspected— that Tim would not have given himself away had he not been so fucking off his face and coaxed into it. He most certainly did not look like he would ever do something like this again.

But I would… if Garrick tells me to.

Callum sighed, embarrassed by this self-admission. What was it about the dark-haired monster that had such an effect on him? Why did he feel the need to share a bed with the man so badly. Callum pulled at his hair and groaned, "Why the fuck am I so keen for you to stay the night?"

"Maybe you're falling in love with me?"

Callum flinched. He looked behind him and saw Garrick walking into the lounge. "Oh my god. Did you just hear me?"

Garrick smiled and nodded.

He blushed, covering his face with his hands. "Fuck my life."

Garrick laughed. "There's plenty of things I like to fuck on you but your life isn't one of them." He crossed the floor and rubbed Callum on the shoulder.

"I didn't think you were coming back."

Garrick tilted his head. "Why wouldn't I come back? You kept your end of the deal, so I am here to meet mine."

"But how come you were gone so long? Tim's folks only live five minutes away."

Garrick didn't respond. He grabbed Callum's hand and dragged him into the kitchen.

When Callum looked at the table he was lost for words, his heart melting. On the table was a terracotta garden tray holding a mix of seedlings and half-grown lettuces and carrots."

"I swung by home and picked this up. I had a spare one in the garage and snuck next door and dug up some of my neighbours veges to help get you started," Garrick said. "You said you wanted to start a garden of your own so..." he smiled and shrugged, "Now you can."

Callum laughed. "You stole plants for me?"

Garrick raised Callum's hand, kissing him softly on the knuckles. "I sure did. And it won't be the last thing I steal either."

"Oh yeah. What's next? A car? money?"

"Something way fucking better than that." Garrick kissed him on the lips and whispered, "Your heart."

Callum's knees went weak. "Wow."

"Wow indeed." Garrick wrapped his arms around Callum's waist, drawing their crotches together. "But I suspect I may already have it." He waggled his eyebrows.

"No you don't," Callum said, his lip quirking.

Garrick laughed. "You're bluffing. Your lip curled up."

Callum's heart fluttered. He felt like his emotions had been stripped bare but he still had enough sense to play it cool. "In your dreams, mate. I am fond of you. Not in love with you."

"I told you. You can't lie to me. I always know if your bluffing." His dark eyes shone with sincerity.

"You sure it isn't a case of me having your heart already," Callum said casually.

"Honestly… I don't know.".

"Typical. Heart of stone, you." Callum smiled, not wanting Garrick to see his disappointment.

"It's not like that, Callum." Garrick bit down on his lip. "It's just that I take stuff like that as it comes." He paused meaningfully, but Callum wasn't sure why. "I don't…" Garrick started, looking away briefly before returning his gaze. "I don't have a heart of stone. I'm not immune from feeling attached to someone. And I am very attached to you."

"Yeah right," Callum mumbled.

Garrick let go of Callum's waist and grabbed hold of his hands, holding them tight. "I am attached to you. That's not a lie. Do you have any idea how jealous I am that Tim is your best mate and not me?"

Callum remained quiet, wanting Garrick to continue.

"It's driven me crazy for ages. Well before tonight. You're the most important person in my world, Callum. You're my best mate, even if I ain't yours."

Callum took a deep breath and pulled his hand away. "If I am such a good mate then how come you've been so horrible the way you… the way you have your way with me."

"I think you're confusing horrible with kinky."

"Am I though?"

"Everyone has a freak streak in them, buddy, mine just happens to be a little darker." Garrick smiled. "Are you saying you don't enjoy the way I fuck you?"

Callum mulled over this for a bit. "I don't know. I don't like everything you do but if I'm being entirely honest then yeah, I guess there are parts of it I enjoy."

Garrick simpered, looking pleased with himself.

"What I wanna know is, why did you make me do stuff with Tim?" Callum shook his head "*That,* I just don't understand."

"Like I said, I have a dark freak streak." He waggled his eyebrows. "And the guy needed being brought down a peg or two."

"What the fuck?" Callum scoffed. "Why would he need that?"

"Because I'm a jealous son of a bitch."

Callum grinned. "A tad possessive, are we?"

"Like you wouldn't believe." Garrick leaned forward and gently kissed his neck. "So would you be keen to do some more experimenting with me?"

"What's in it for me?"

"I dunno. I can't promise anything. I could give you the world or end up breaking your heart."

"Not much incentive then is there."

"That's the thing with love. It's all a risk." Garrick gave a winsome smile. "Are you prepared to be a risk taker and find out?"

Risk. It always came back to taking a fucking risk. It didn't go unnoticed by Callum that history was repeating itself. They were standing in the very spot Misty had been when she told Callum two years earlier that she was leaving because of his aversion to risk. He looked at the incredibly beautiful man in front of him. A man who was jealous of his friendship with Tim, a man who was attached to him but couldn't guarantee his heart. Was this a risk worth taking?

Callum sighed, his emotions breaking through. "I'm scared, though. Really fucking scared." He fought back tears welling in his eyes. "Sorry. I know I probably sound like a scared little boy."

"Don't be stupid. Even grown men are allowed to be scared," Garrick said firmly. He rubbed Callum's cheek with his thumb. "You're the last guy I'd say behaves like a little boy."

"Really?"

"You're a good man, Callum Bradshaw. And a rather-fucking-wonderful human being."

Misty's harsh words which had felt like gospel, suddenly felt little more than crazy cult ramblings. The tears in his eyes broke through, rolling down in a mix of relief and joy.

"And you don't need to be scared," Garrick whispered.

"Why not?" Callum snivelled.

"Because you're not alone on this one." Garrick kissed away the tears running down his cheeks. "We will be taking the risk together."

The way he said it made Callum feel more at ease. Yes, it was all a risk, but Garrick was right. They would be taking it together.

"So where exactly is this risk taking us?" Callum asked.

Garrick smiled, thinking it over. "Right now… it is taking us to your bedroom, *babe*." He placed his lips to Callum's, locking them together in a tongue-laced kiss.

When they unlocked their mouths, Callum couldn't wipe the smile from his face. A fresh force of hope flowed through his veins.

Hand in hand, they wandered to the bedroom, stepping in a new direction.

Taking a risk.

EPILOGUE

Callum sat in his majestic tree, looking out at the beautiful land of his dreams. It was nice here. It really was. He gazed ahead at the snow-capped mountains and the valleys of sparkling blue rivers. Perfect sunny skies shone above and he could hear the soundtrack of nature singing below.

But just like every other time, it didn't last. The storm clouds rolled in like a steam train and a pungent whiff of smoke snuck up Callum's nostrils, alerting him to a fiery furnace below. He peered down, discovering the monstrous flames racing up the tree's limbs like demonic racing cars. He stood away from the billowing smoke, trying to get fresh air into his lungs.

He knew what he had to do, he knew he had to escape. He half-expected to become frozen in fear, too scared to leave his sanctuary. But instead of panicking, worried about the smoke and scorching heat, Callum just smiled. He wasn't scared anymore.

Stepping off was just a slight risk compared to what he knew he was capable of in the land of the awake. The thin veil separating sleep and dreams was just that. *Thin.* No matter what happened here, he knew that once he woke up, he wouldn't be alone. He would have a beautiful man laying beside him with strong arms that knew how to fight and protect. The same beautiful man who had cradled Callum to sleep, cuddling and kissing him like their naked bodies together was the most natural thing in the world. Nothing wrong or forbidden about it.

Callum stepped towards the edge of his skyscraper tree. He looked down at the ginormous drop to the forest floor. He wasn't sure if he would grow wings, he wasn't sure if he could fly. But that didn't really matter now. He knew Garrick would be there to catch him.

"Fuck it," he said, stepping off and shooting his fear in the face.

His body fell, hurling at a velocity of lightning speed, the rush of wind lashing his face. The fall became faster and faster, the forest floor getting closer and closer.

But he still wasn't scared.

He waited. He waited for an outcome. And just at the final moment, milliseconds away from splatting on the ground, he grew invisible wings and was saved from danger. A whoosh of victory swept over him. He had defeated his demons.

His spirit climbed high, high, high into the sky, flying and zooming along like a spectacular energy. There was no crying, no screaming—just smiling.

Callum opened his eyes, finding himself safe and well in his own bedroom. His body tingled with what he could only describe as love. He let his sight drift over Garrick who was fast asleep on his side with an arm draped around Callum's waist, holding him in close.

Callum pressed his lips to his lover's warm skin, kissing the light scars on Garrick's chest—the only part on the man that was free of perfection and probably the most beautiful. Callum's own scars were on the inside, but he prayed that Garrick would consider them his most beautiful feature too.

Garrick looked so sexy curled up the way he was. Even the way he slept was sexy. Deep, peaceful exhales that sounded beautiful.

Beautiful. Everything about him.

"*Him*," Callum whispered. It didn't sound masculine or feminine anymore, it just sounded right. He clutched Garrick's strong protective arm. The arm of Callum's lover and *best mate*.

Callum may have been laying still, but he felt like he was moving... *moving on*. Garrick had helped him change, take chances, show some sponta-fucking-neity and reminded him he was a man. A good man.

He closed his eyes and nuzzled into Garrick's chest to go back to sleep. Callum was ready for whatever life threw at him—asleep or awake. If he was brave enough to take risks then there would never be a nightmare too scary to stop him from waking up beside a dream come true.

The beginning...

Zane Menzy

THANK YOU

Thank you so much for taking the time out to read Game Night. There is an ocean of books available to readers so it means a lot to me that you chose to read mine.

Zane

About the Author

Zane lives way down under on the west coast of beautiful New Zealand; the wet side. He is a fan of ghost stories, music, sport, ducklings and nights out that usually lead to his head hanging in a bucket the next morning.

He enjoys creating characters who have flaws, crazy thoughts and a tendency to make bad decisions. His stories range from steamy romantic adventures to inspirational romance.

Zane Menzy

Game Night

Made in the USA
Middletown, DE
12 March 2018